A Rugged Beauty

LACY WILLIAMS

One

THE WOMAN WOKE up to the feeling of something tickling her cheek.

When she opened her eyes, pain like a broad needle pierced inside her skull. She closed her eyes, but the pain persisted as a throbbing drum.

Little by little, it abated to a dull ache that seemed to echo the beating of her heart.

This time, she cracked her eyes first.

How much time had passed since that first awareness? She didn't know, but now a faint shadow fell over her face. She squinted and registered the small, even leaves of a box elder sheltering her from the sunlight.

She was outdoors.

But where was she?

Her stomach twisted violently as she pushed up on one elbow, and then to a sitting position. Somehow she knew there was nothing inside her empty belly. She pressed one hand against her midsection and tried to breathe. Her mouth felt as parched as a preacher's tongue after a long-winded sermon.

Something was wrong. She was sure of it, even as the ringing in her ears cleared away and was replaced by a bird chirping from somewhere nearby.

Scanning all directions, the unsettled feeling persisted. She seemed to be sitting beneath a copse of trees. The soft breeze and warm air might indicate it was summer. Beyond the trees and some undergrowth, there was only emptiness. As if the land was one vast prairie.

Her stomach lurched, but this time from nerves.

The sense of wrongness solidified, and she realized she could not remember her own name.

She turned her hand in front of her face, searching the light brown skin as if the shaking appendage could unlock the answer for her.

The more she pressed her mind, the bigger her headache grew. Fragments of... memories?... what must be memories pressed behind her eyes.

Her... brother. Yes!

Remembered affection flowed through her, along with relief, as her mind showed her images of a young man with black hair and laughing dark brown eyes.

Her mouth tried to form a word—his name—but the information stayed just out of reach as the pounding in her head grew so intense that she could no longer chase the thought-memory and it slipped away.

She did not know her own name. Or her brother's.

Nor why she was outdoors in the middle of an echoing wilderness.

The blue gingham dress and dirt-smudged apron were

unfamiliar to her as she patted the fabric and searched her pockets for any clue and found none.

She pushed one hand into the springy curls of her damp hair. A trickling of water nearby registered, as did a terrifying memory of being submerged beneath surging water. The memory only lasted as long as her blink, but for that fractured second she felt trapped in a vortex of water and her body sucked in a breath to dispel the image.

What had happened? Something terrible. It must have been terrible if she was out here alone.

Was she alone?

Her brain felt sluggish and hazy but the thought lodged and stuck.

"H-hello?" Was that her voice, feeble and raspy? Had it carried any farther than the box elder standing sentinel?

Speaking reminded her of the dryness in her throat and mouth. She was so thirsty and the trickle of water rushed and rushed in her head until it was all she could hear.

Her head pounded again when she forced her shaking legs to stand, but she made it to her feet. What had happened to her?

One wobbly step, then another. Something caught her eye on the ground... it looked like someone had vomited—

Another glance encompassed where she had been lying in proximity to the sick mottling the ground strewn with decaying leaves.

Oh. *She* had been sick.

That explained the gnawing emptiness in her stomach, the dryness in her mouth, the thirst.

But it did not explain why she couldn't remember anything before waking up.

Her body could no longer deny the need for water,

even to answer the growing questions in her mind and she took several shaky steps before she needed to lean one hand against a sapling to steady herself.

A few more steps and she emerged from the cover of the trees. She squinted in bright sunlight. Morning still, but barely.

There was the water. A wide swath of river, sparkling like diamonds as it passed over a bed of smooth, round rocks. Farther down, the water narrowed in a bend, rushing over large boulders.

Moving quickly now, the woman crossed the expanse of damp gravel, her feet twisting beneath her as the ground shifted.

She knelt at the edge of the river, uncaring that her dress got wet, that her knees chilled at the icy shock.

She cupped her hands and drank handful after handful of fresh water so cold it made her teeth ache.

Breathless but finally sated, she sat back on her haunches. Her eyes roamed in all directions.

She didn't know what she was looking for. A house. A town. Smoke. Horses. Any sign of civilization. Any sign that she wasn't completely alone.

There was only the expanse of blue sky, littered with clouds.

Fear slithered through her like smoke filtering through cracks in a smokeshack.

"Help!" Her voice cracked on the word, but it didn't stop her from shouting, "Is anyone there? Help! Heeellp!"

But it was as if the wind snatched her voice. No one answered.

The water had healed her parched throat enough that the twist in her stomach felt like hunger.

Surely she wasn't alone out here. There must be something. A house. A tent.

Her nose twitched and she turned her head, searching for the faintest hint of woodsmoke. Was she imagining it?

Heart pounding, her feet led her back the way she'd come, into the woods.

Yards away, a dark shape loomed. And jerked.

She shrieked and stopped short, pressing one hand to her chest. How had she not noticed it before? A man's coat, some kind of slicker, hung from a branch well above her head. Another gust of the breeze set it twisting and swaying.

Someone was out here.

Were they friend or foe?

The scent of smoke was slightly stronger here, a fire long burned away. Her heart quailed as she circled around the coat, sleeves flapping in the breeze. She noticed a small campfire, only ashes and a few black lumps of charred wood. No tent. No shovel or clothesline or hammer.

She'd camped with her father when she was young. The thought was quickly followed by a sense of urgency as she tried to picture his face in her memories. No matter how hard she tried to force him to come in to focus, she couldn't remember.

This was only a dead campfire, not a camp.

What now?

She pressed the heels of both hands to her eyes. Why couldn't she remember? The rising panic inside her clawed its way up her throat, but she couldn't let it out. Some instinct told her that breaking down in tears at this moment was dangerous.

She'd grown up in the city. That knowledge clicked

into place with a certainty that had to be real. She could've navigated home from the grocers or the butcher or her friend Flora's house.

Flora.

The name settled in place, too. Along with a clear memory of a young girl with medium brown skin with copper undertones and her hair in a kerchief. Sparkling, mischievous eyes.

Flora.

But when the woman tried to ask her memory-friend what her own name was, the memory faded.

If the woman was comfortable in the city, what was she doing out on this prairie, alone?

The man's coat beckoned as if it could answer.

Again the thought stuck. Maybe she wasn't alone.

"H-hello?" she called out softly.

A noise came from deeper in the woods, a breaking branch. The woman wheeled and strained her eyes to see, but only the wind rustled the leaves.

Something shifted to her left. What she'd taken for a part of the landscape, a brown mass, moved.

A man.

He wore pants the color of earth, and a shirt, once white, now streaked with mud. That's why she had thought him part of the ground.

A slight groan spilled from him as he rolled from where he'd curled around himself to splay flat on his back. His skin was darker than hers, a rich brown. From several feet away, she saw his hands were used to work, calloused and strong.

Who was he? His face was turned from her. A hat lay several feet beyond him.

Again she wondered, friend or foe?

She didn't know the answer.

And then his head turned. When he opened his eyes, he was looking right at her.

* * *

The man had only a moment to notice the young woman's wide, shocked eyes. Dark eyes. Her hair caught up behind her head, though wisps of curls framed her face. Her dress and the apron she wore over it wrinkled as if they had been soaked and dried while crumpled in a ball. Her tawny skin was kissed with a faint undertone of pink, as if she had been out in the sun too long.

Something tugged at him, a pull of familiarity that seemed at odds with the suspicious narrowing of her eyes.

"Who are you?" she demanded.

Then a pause, the length of one heartbeat. He didn't know the answer to her question.

"Who are you?" he countered.

She was hovering behind a fallen, decaying tree as if she feared him, though he remained flat on the ground.

"I asked you first." The tilt of her chin that might mean stubbornness. Yes. Stubborn.

He felt an ache at the base of his skull, and when he raised one hand to rub it, she flinched. The pain bloomed and expanded to a dull roar in his head.

"Did you poison me?" Something in his throat and mouth tasted wrong. His body felt weak, a feeling he associated with surviving a fatiguing fever.

The narrowing of her eyes intensified, a frown pulling at her mouth. He had one stray thought that her features weren't used to the expression. How could he know that about her, when he didn't even know her name? Or his own?

"If I did, I poisoned the both of us." Her mouth took on a determined slant. "I can't remember a thing," she admitted softly.

That was not good. He didn't know how they had come to be here, wherever here was. And he didn't know this woman.

When he sat up, she took several shuffling steps backward.

He took in the campfire, now cold. A quick glance around the small clearing showed no other supplies.

"There's nothing here," she said, as if her thoughts had followed his gaze around the clearing. "No house. No city. No wagon or horses to pull it."

"It'd be oxen you'd want for a long journey." The words slipped past his lips before a conscious thought had formed.

Her brows furrowed above intelligent eyes. "How do you know that?"

He shook his head, but aborted the movement and winced as pain spiked behind his eyes. "I don't know how I know it, I just do."

She crossed her arms over her midsection. "It's like we've been dropped from the sky in this wilderness."

Though his head protested, he forced himself to his feet. Wobbled a bit, but that passed when he spread his feet wide.

"Fanciful," he said. "But not possible. There has to be an explanation."

Her lips pursed and for a moment, he was caught in a staring contest, wariness exuding from both sides.

She was beautiful. There was no denying it. When he would've acted on the tug in his gut pulling him toward her, she glanced to the side, giving him her profile.

"You don't remember anything?" he prodded.

He took a couple of steps to reach the fire and nudged the toe of his boot through the ashes. It was completely dead, completely cold. It could've been out for hours. Or days, though that seemed less likely because the ashes weren't scattered.

"I remember the name of a little girl I knew when I was a child... I think. My brother's face. My father is just a faint trace..."

Her words prompted memory of a child's laughter, then a terrified shriek, though he received no images to go along with the sounds.

When he went to put his hands on his hips, he felt the leather belt around his waist. He glanced down as his fingertips explored.

A gun belt, though there weren't any bullets in the small leather holes made for such. Still, a revolver rested in its holster.

The man's hand closed over the gun's stock for a brief moment. He felt a sense of rightness, of security. He was meant to have this weapon, for protection. But he couldn't say why.

He patted his hips, and then his breast pocket. Empty.

When he looked up, she was watching him closely.

The awareness made heat rise in his face. "I don't suppose you've got anything useful in your pockets? Like a family Bible inscribed with our names?"

Something shifted in her expression. "Do you think our names would be in the same Bible?" A pause, a caught breath.

Married. That's what it would likely mean to find their names were inscribed in a family Bible.

The uncertainty in her expression magnified.

"I do know you somehow." He hadn't meant to say the words, but there they were. He'd wanted to ease her fear, and they were true. He knew her. He felt it. He just didn't know how.

She nodded toward something behind him. "There's a coat hanging."

When he twisted to see, she continued, "It's much too big to fit me. It must be yours."

It only took a few strides to reach where it hung in the tree. He pulled it down, feeling a lingering dampness at the seams.

"How come I'm not wearing it?"

She shrugged helplessly.

He reached into the pockets, came up empty. Disappointment rankled.

But as he folded the garment over his arm, something heavy thunked against his side. He examined the coat again, this time finding the inside breast pocket. Its flap was tucked closed. Inside, more moisture.

"It's possible we took a swim." His conclusion made her brows wrinkle again. "The inside of this pocket is wet. And your dress had to have been soaked at some point."

She looked down at herself.

His fingers closed over something cool and rectangular —he drew out a small leather bound book, tied with a leather thong.

He flipped the book open. Reading the words sliced pain through his skull.

Numbers. Columns of numbers, scribbled... names? An occasional sketch in the corner of one page.

Independence Rock. Fort Bridger. *Ten lost.*

He couldn't make sense of it. Nor the sense of urgency that stole over him. *Hurry.*

"It's a log book," he said absently, still flipping through the pages. "I can't understand it."

It would've been more helpful to have found a diary or journal. Not ... whatever this was.

"What use is a log book?" she asked, the question an echo of his own musings.

It stirred the muddy soup of his thoughts. "A traveler might use it."

The words settled deep. Yes. A traveler. *He* was a traveler. But when he pushed for more answers from inside himself, there was only a dark void. A punch of fear. *Run!* The voice from somewhere inside that darkness seemed almost audible.

He blinked, and the charged moment—memory?—faded.

"If we are travelers, where are our belongings? Those oxen you mentioned? Friends or others we might've traveled with?" There was a building desperation in her voice.

He didn't have any answers to calm her. "I don't know. You're right. We wouldn't have come out here alone."

"What if we are lost?" she whispered.

Two

ALICE SPENCER SCRUBBED a pair of dark blue pants over the washboard across the tub. The suds in the water had developed a brown hue so she figured this washtub was only good for one or two more items of clothing.

Her lower back ached. Her knees felt every inch of the hard-packed earth beneath them as she knelt over the tub of water she'd lugged from the nearby creek to the circle of wagons. But it was her heart that felt sick.

They'd camped in this same spot for two days as search party after search party had been sent out to locate Hollis Tremblay and Abigail Fletcher. Both the wagon master and the young woman had disappeared after a river crossing two days ago, and the captains of their Oregon-bound train had refused to move on until the two were found.

Abigail's wagon had been abandoned on the bank of the river, the oxen still in their traces. But there was no sign of either person, or of Hollis's horse. Alice was worried for her friend. And for the rest of the pioneers who'd come west under Hollis's leadership.

Tensions had escalated in camp. Even so, the work never seemed to end.

A bubble landed on Alice's cheek. She rubbed it against her shoulder. The motion caused a strand of russet hair to fall from its pins right into her eyes. She blew air straight up, not willing to get soapy water all over her face.

"I'm fine." Alice's sister-in-law Stella stood at the back of her nearby conestoga wagon.

"You don't look fine," Alice's brother Collin, Stella's husband, said.

He was right.

Stella was one of the toughest women Alice had ever met. For several weeks after the Oregon-bound train had pulled out from Independence, Missouri, Stella had dressed and acted like a man. She'd joined hunting parties, worked as hard as any man in their company.

But right now, she was as pale as a brand-new handkerchief. Her eyes were glassy.

Collin had his back to Alice, but she could guess just how his brows wrinkled in concern.

"Why don't you lie down for a bit? I'll fetch Maddie and she can check you over."

Collin's left hand cupped Stella's elbow. His wife leaned into him, her body language showing relief as his arm slid around her waist.

Alice wrung out the pair of pants with a mite too much force and splattered water on her skirt.

"You need any help?"

Coop, Collin's twin and Alice's youngest brother,

appeared from outside the ring of wagons, coffee cup in hand, and moved to squat next to her.

Alice used the back of her wrist to wipe her brow, that one strand of hair still tickling her nose.

"I'll manage," she murmured.

She flipped the next item—the last one, thank the Lord—into the sudsy water and stole the coffee cup right out of her brother's hand.

"Hey." His protest was weak. Almost as weak as the coffee. Alice made a face and handed him back the cup.

She plunged her hands into the water, swirling the shirt to soak it.

Coop nodded to Collin and Stella. "Think she's in the family way?"

Alice's eyes darted to where Collin had his arm around his wife. Something hot and prickly lodged behind her sternum. She pulled the sopping shirt out of the water and began rubbing it over the washboard. Drops of water scattered everywhere. Coop's brows went up.

"It's early," she muttered to the board. Collin and Stella had only been married a few weeks, after he'd discovered her true identity and they'd fallen for each other.

"She's been poorly the last couple mornings," Coop said.

Alice shook her head. "She could've eaten something that didn't agree with her."

The first two weeks on the trail, Alice's stomach had been off. She'd blamed food, cooked over a campfire. But maybe it was more than that. Alice's entire life had been upended to take this journey west.

"Blech."

She glanced up at Coop's groan and caught Collin's quick peck against Stella's lips.

"Now I'm the one feeling ill," Coop muttered.

Alice's stomach had knotted at the affectionate gesture. She didn't begrudge her brother his happiness. Or Leo, her older brother, either. Even their half-brothers, August and Owen Mason, had found happiness on the wagon train.

Alice was happy for all of them. She liked their wives—even Rachel, who'd been an acquired taste. But Alice had thought she would be the first one in their family to settle down. To marry. To have children.

She'd been horribly wrong.

It had to be ironic that Robert Braddock chose that moment to cross between two campfires on the far side of the circled wagons.

The man was tall, broad-shouldered. His hat had once been white, but it was stained and dented now. His fancy duds hadn't fared well on the trail, either. She saw the hole —unpatched—in the knee of his pants. The old Alice, the one who'd still had dreams, would've worried that he wasn't eating, or taking care of himself.

He wasn't looking her direction.

She was a foolish girl to give him even one moment of her thoughts.

Just before she steeled herself to look away, Alice saw his hand flex at his side.

No. His thumb and forefinger formed a circle, other fingers spread wide.

He wanted to meet.

It was their special signal. Or it had been, once upon a time.

Her knuckles scraped against the washboard. She

gasped and looked down at the same time. Pulling her stinging hand out of the tub. Her knuckles were raw and pink.

"What happened?" Coop asked.

"Wasn't paying attention."

She'd let herself be distracted by Braddock. Something hot burned behind her nose and she flared her nostrils, afraid of the questions if a tear slipped free.

Or maybe afraid to give in to the emotions. She stuffed them down where they belonged, in a dark box deep inside her. A coffin.

She wouldn't meet him again. Not ever.

When she turned her head sharply, so that Braddock wasn't even in her line of sight, she got a whiff of whiskey.

Surely that wasn't coming from her brother.

She squinted at Coop, grateful for the reprieve, even if it meant focusing on another problem.

"Give me your shirt," she demanded.

Coop instantly looked as if he would refuse.

"There's a clean one in the wagon," she said. "You've been wearing that one for three days."

He begrudgingly put down his coffee cup and unbuttoned the top of his shirt before he reached behind him and pulled the entire thing over his head. She snatched it from his hands before he could dunk it in the water. Pressed it to her face and breathed in deeply.

The whiskey scent was faint, barely noticeable. Was he imbibing again?

Coop watched her with stormy eyes, surely realizing what she'd done.

She dunked the shirt into the water, unapologetic.

Her brother had promised that he would stop drinking. He'd given his word the last time she'd caught him with a silver flask in his hand.

But he'd made other promises before. Disappointment sat bitter in her throat.

Footsteps approached. She glanced up.

Braddock, only feet away.

Alice stood on shaky legs, aware of Coop as he straightened beside her. Her brother was already bristling.

"I need to talk to you." Braddock stared right at her as he said the words.

"Go away," Coop said.

Had he even noticed how Braddock looked at her?

"If you won't come to me—"

Now Alice felt the weight of Coop's glance between her and Braddock. She didn't look at her brother, though she couldn't hold Braddock's gaze either.

"She's got nothing to say to you."

At Coop's words, Braddock looked at him for the first time. "I'm not talking to you." The disdain in his voice was clear, an echo of what she'd heard months ago, when Braddock had spoken other words.

Alice looked over her shoulder, but Collin and Stella were gone.

Coop took a step toward Braddock, putting himself in arms' reach. "You stay away from my sister," he growled.

"Maybe you should stay away from her," Braddock said. "You're the reason she's out here working herself into a shadow—"

Coop swung at him.

Braddock must've seen the punch coming, because he moved to the side. The punch connected with his shoulder instead of his face. He threw himself at Coop, taking a blow to his side. Braddock grunted.

"Stop it!" Alice cried. Fighting wasn't allowed in the company, and Coop had been in enough trouble on the early days of their journey.

Braddock threw an awkward elbow and Coop retaliated with a shove that sent Braddock stumbling back two steps. His hat fell off and his hair was tousled.

"That's enough." Alice's voice trembled. Did either of them even hear her? They stared at each other like two dogs about to pounce.

"Come on," Coop motioned Braddock toward him. "You're a lousy fighter. I'll teach you how to take a whooping."

She'd seen that look of determination on Braddock's face before.

"Stop it, Coop," she demanded.

But Braddock had already stepped toward her brother.

She jumped forward and grabbed for Coop's left arm. He must've seen her from the corner of his eye because he gave a shove—and it sent her sprawling.

For a fractured second, Coop turned to look at her with shock and remorse.

It was just long enough for Braddock to roar and swing —and connect with Coop's jaw.

Her brother put his hands on his knees for a brief moment and then rounded on Braddock, punching his face.

Alice heard the smack of Coop's fist on flesh as she scrambled to her feet.

Again and again Coop struck.

Braddock had been knocked to the ground, but that didn't stop Coop.

Alice shrieked for her brother to let up, but just before she jumped on his back to force him, another voice called out, "Coop!"

Leo.

For a prolonged moment, she thought Coop would keep beating on Braddock, but he pulled back. Alice hadn't realized she was crying until she pressed her hands to her cheeks and they came away wet.

Braddock lay prone on the ground as Leo dragged Coop away. Blood poured from the lip of the man she'd once loved. He clutched his stomach.

Part of her wanted to help him. But she saw Leo's furious look and the red scrape blooming on Coop's jaw and remembered she'd promised herself never to speak to Braddock again.

She turned and left.

* * *

What if we are lost out here?

The woman's words plopped into the center of the man's mind, landing and then rippling like a rock tossed in a calm pond.

"If we are lost, then someone will come looking for us." His words emerged with more calm than he felt.

Ten lost.

The words had been written at the top of one of the last pages of the book he'd flipped through. He didn't know what they meant, only the sinking feeling that had come over him when he'd read the words.

Ten cows?

Ten children?

Ten days?

Surely they hadn't been out here alone for ten days.

"Do you really think someone is looking for us?" Her voice held a trembling hope.

He hated to quash it. "I don't know. I'd like to figure out what happened—"

"How can we, if we can't remember anything? We don't even know our own names."

He motioned to the cold ashes. "We can look for clues, try to think backward and deduce what happened. It might help us figure out where we are and who might be looking for us."

He circled the fire, which sent him in her direction. He was trying hard to ignore the pounding headache at the base of his skull and almost missed the way she shifted at his movement. Like she was frightened of him. He didn't miss the calculating way she looked at him, the intelligence shining in her eyes.

"I'm going to walk around in circles small to large," he explained.

"I'll go down to the river." She cleared her throat when her voice emerged small. "See what I can find there."

He didn't miss the look she sent over her shoulder as she marched away.

It couldn't be more clear that she didn't trust him. The more he pushed his brain for some clear information, other than the general sense of familiarity and warmth toward her, he got only a blank emptiness.

He widened his circles, constantly scanning the ground and bushes and trees. Looking for anything that might help him figure out what was going on. A hoof print. Leaves or grass disturbed.

There.

Beneath the place where he'd removed his—his?—slicker from the tree branch, a pocketknife lay on the ground. He slipped it into his pocket. It'd probably fallen from the coat. It was a little thing, but the tool could prove helpful.

The man's stomach rumbled uneasily. He couldn't quite tell whether he was hungry or sick.

Another circle revealed a mess of vomit not far from where the man had woken on the ground. He'd been sick, then. He squatted to examine it more closely. He used a twig from the ground nearby to shift some of the mess. Those looked like masticated berries—

He heard the rustle of the woman's skirt as she moved through the brush. She was yards away now, though not at the river's edge yet.

She bent to reach for something, knee-height. Leaves on a bush rattled and some instinct screamed at him as he watched her considering something she'd plucked from the bush.

He stood and jogged several feet in her direction as her hand moved toward her mouth.

"Don't eat that!" He put more force behind the words than he intended and she jumped, something spilling from her hands.

As he neared, he saw the small purple berries rolling on the leaf-strewn ground.

The woman's eyes were large in her face, and she backed up a step as he approached. He stopped, not wanting to frighten her worse than he already had.

"Something made us sick," he told her. He jerked his thumb over his shoulder where he'd left the vomit behind. "There are berries, pieces of them, in the—the sick."

Her face had lost some of its color. "They look like blueberries, don't they? Surely a berry wouldn't have poisoned us..."

He shook his head. His stomach ached in some remembered warning. "Don't eat the berries. Maybe your belly is as empty as mine, but we can't risk falling sick out here—again." It hadn't hit him until just this moment how vulnerable he'd been—they'd been?—lying out in the open. In broad daylight.

What if someone with nefarious intentions had stumbled on them? What if a wild animal had come sniffing?

She opened her mouth, and he *knew* that she was on the verge of arguing with him.

"Don't." The command in his voice was audible, and even though he'd meant only to protect her, she snapped her mouth closed and her eyes narrowed in suspicion.

But she left the bush behind and moved toward the river.

He kept one eye on her as he resumed his search in ever-widening circles.

When he reached the bank of the river, a good distance from where she stood, he began to put the pieces together.

Upstream, the water rushed. Here in this bend, it pooled deeply, but the banks widened just beyond.

There were cuts in the mud, dry summer grass trampled and smaller bushes dismantled. Like someone—or two someones—desperate to escape the river had pulled themselves out of the water as quickly as possible. The large spots of flattened grass might indicate they'd laid there for a long time. Recovering?

He looked upstream where rapids flowed with white foam. The dangerous rocks, the fast-moving water. It'd be easy to get caught on something underwater and drown.

For a moment, his mind pictured a fragment of swirling water choking him, dragging him by the boots.

He blinked and the image was gone. Was it real? Something he'd experienced? Or a figment of his imagination?

If they'd been swept away by the river, it was a miracle they'd survived.

He moved from the river's edge in a slow circuit back to where the campfire had been. Caught sight of two or three broken twigs where the two of them might've brushed against a bush or tree while they'd walked.

There was nothing else. No hoof print. No boot prints that didn't match his or her dainty footprint.

Thirst drove him back to the river, though he kept to the shallows. She sat on a wide, flat rock, worrying one corner of her apron between her fingers while sunshine bathed her head and shoulders.

He squatted and brought water to his mouth in cupped hands. The moment it hit his empty stomach, the water threatened to come right back up. He breathed deeply through his nose and finally, his stomach settled.

He stayed in his squat, eyes on the water, as his disjointed thoughts tumbled. Then he pulled the little book from his pocket and untied it.

He flipped through the pages more slowly this time. Names of places, number of miles. Some notes on the landscape or game animals. At the bottom corner of one page was a sketch of a wild bird. A grouse, his memory supplied.

It was no help. Not unless he could remember what the names meant. Where was he going?

Or maybe this wasn't even his book.

He tied it closed and put it in his pocket. When his fingers brushed against the knife, he pulled it out of his pocket. Turned it over in his hands.

The initials H.T. had been carved into the handle.

"What's that?" she called out.

"Knife. I found it where the slicker was hanging. It's got a set of initials on it."

She wrinkled her nose when he told her what they were.

"It was too much to hope that you'd recognize if they belonged to me," he said.

"Should I call you H?"

He shrugged. "I don't even know whether it's my coat. My knife."

She stayed on her rock, the sparkling water sending rays of light shining off her skin in reflection. "Is there anything we do know?"

He told her his best guess: that they'd been swept downstream, that they'd tried to dry off by the fire and eaten berries at some point.

Her shoulders straightened. "If we were swept downstream, does that mean we could follow the river back... somewhere?"

He straightened and rubbed his forehead beneath his hat.

"The safest thing to do is to stay where we are," he said. "And wait to be found."

She frowned so big he could see it from where he stood.

"That doesn't feel very safe." Her words were barely audible over the babbling water flowing over stones. She pressed one hand against her stomach. Was she having the same hunger pangs he was?

They needed sustenance.

Run!

That voice in his head echoed again. Was it a child's voice? Without any context, he couldn't be certain.

Unease swamped him. They needed shelter. They needed help. But he caught another wary gaze from the woman.

They wouldn't survive out here without trusting each other.

The woman felt another shiver of awareness from where she knelt over the carefully constructed pile of fine twigs and some thin, dry grasses the man had provided. He wasn't trying to be quiet as he dragged several branches through the woods to construct a shelter not far away. He'd collected several larger tree branches and broken off the twigs. Now he was forming a semi-circle around a tree with the branches, though he'd only made one partial wall so far.

He didn't speak or glance her way as he upended one of the branches he'd dragged near and added it to the growing shelter. She wished she knew whether his silence was normal. Or anything about him.

He'd startled her on his first trip back to the tree. He'd been carrying the limbs and she didn't know how a man so big could walk so quietly. She'd been bent over her pile of twigs, trying to ignite a spark when he'd seemed to have come out of nowhere.

She wasn't proud of it, but she'd shrieked in terror.

There was no mistaking the look of hurt he'd sent her before he'd carefully blanked his expression.

He'd made several more trips since, being noisy and dragging branches everywhere.

The sun was setting, hidden by a ridge beyond the river. It wasn't dark yet, but the light was fading fast. Urgency spurred her on as she handled the stick her companion had smoothed out with his knife before creating a pointed end. He'd carved a rough bowl from a flat piece of bark and left her with both pieces. Now she fitted the pointed end into the bowl and placed both hands flat together with the stick between them.

Familiarity crept over her at the motion and something, not quite a memory, rose up inside of her. Slowly, she rolled her hands back and forth so that the stick rotated between them.

She kept at it for several moments, a creeping feeling telling her this was right.

When she removed the pointed stick and touched one finger inside the bowl, it was warm enough that she jerked her finger back.

Instinct had her gathering a pinch of the dried grasses and adding it to the bowl. She put the stick back and twisted it more. Faster.

When a tiny spark glowed, she dropped the stick and bent low to the ground to blow on it—and blew hard enough that the grass flew out of the bowl. By the time it hit the ground, the spark had gone out.

But she'd made one spark. She could make another.

She was placing a new bit of grass carefully in the bowl when the man dragged another set of branches into sight.

"I know this." Excitement made her slightly careless as she tossed the words toward him. "I've done this before. Made a fire just like this."

She saw his half smile as he fitted the branch into place. "That's lucky for us. I figured you for a bright woman."

She stalled out, holding on to the pointed stick, when she got a good look at his shelter.

"It's smaller than I thought," she murmured.

He pushed the top of the branch into place, somehow weaving it between two others from the opposite side. She didn't see how the entire thing didn't come tumbling down.

The space between the bottom of the branches, the bottom of the cone, and the base of the tree was narrow. Certainly not big enough for both of them to fit without touching.

Her stomach took a tumble.

"I'll sleep outside. By the fire." His words were calm and untroubled.

She felt the brush of the breeze against her cheek, how cool it'd become as the sun disappeared behind the horizon.

"Do you think we belong together?" She hadn't meant to blurt out the words, but the set of his shoulders and the way he'd turned his face away had affected her somehow.

He looked back at her in surprise, his eyes intent and searching. She dropped her gaze. "I-I mean... do you think we know each other. Since we're—"

"The only two people within several miles?" There was

a hint of humor to his words and it eased the discomfort, allowed her shoulders to drop and relax.

"There's a good chance we know each other," he said the words easily. "We must've been traveling together if we both got swept away at the same time."

Traveling together.

Her hands trembled and she couldn't quite hold his gaze, but she raised her chin. "Then do you think... do you think we're married?"

She hadn't been able to think of anything else since he'd blurted out the idea about a family Bible.

Something flitted across his expression, so quickly she couldn't read it in the fading light.

"It'd be a blessing to be married to someone as beautiful and resourceful as you." For a stark second, it seemed as if the words had surprised him. They certainly had surprised her.

And then he ducked his head and kept working with the shelter. He cleared his throat. "It seems likely we should be. To be so far from any town, on our own..."

She'd had the thought more than once during the afternoon. If only she could remember!

He moved a step toward her and she couldn't keep her gaze from jumping up to clash with his dark eyes. He stopped. Sighed. Knocked his hat off with one hand while he ran the other over his closely-cropped hair.

"Whatever we are to each other, you're safe with me."

She *had* hurt him with her distrust.

"I believe you." The words slipped from her tongue before she'd really thought them through, but she meant them. The realization of how deeply she meant them came after they were spoken.

Something that might be relief flickered through his eyes. "You need help with that?"

She shook her head.

"I figure two more loads and your shelter will be the best it can be for tonight."

The air felt different between them with his statement and her acceptance.

She worked with the pointed stick once more, this time keeping her excitement in check until she had a big, bright, glowing spark that ate away at the bark-fluff.

She carried it in cupped hands to the little patch of twigs and more fluff and within moments, a tiny flame flared to life.

Whatever knowledge was hiding behind the blank darkness of her memory, it prodded her to slowly feed bigger and bigger sticks until she had a merry fire crackling just as the man stood from where he'd knelt as he layered evergreen branches over the back of the shelter.

"Good work," he praised.

She sat back on her heels as warmth from the fire licked her face and neck.

When the man came close and stretched out his hand in offer, she took it. He steadied her as she stood. The clasp of his hand over hers was warm and calloused. She raised her eyes to meet his gaze and for a breathless moment, she stood close enough to embrace him.

He was the one who stepped back. He dropped her hand and for a moment, she missed his warm touch.

"If you want, I can bring some boughs for the ground inside."

She glanced at the space inside the shelter. "Thank you, H."

Surprise flitted across his expression.

She shifted her feet. "I hope it's all right—"

He nodded. "It works. But what should I call you?"

She reached for a name. Anything. But her mind was all darkness and shadows. She shrugged, wrapping her arms around her middle as the helpless, panicky feeling returned.

"Brown-Eyes will have to do for now," he murmured.

She wrinkled her nose. "You have brown eyes, too."

One corner of his mouth tipped. "I could simply go with Beautiful."

Heat suffused her cheeks and she ducked her head. Thankfully, her stomach gurgled, breaking the awkward silence growing between them.

His brows drew together in concern. She glanced at the weapon on his hip. "Can you hunt?"

He followed her gaze and his hand reflexively came to rest on the gun before he dropped it. "Not well, not with a revolver like this." His forehead wrinkled. "I don't know how I know it, only that I do. And there's limited ammunition. Better to save it."

Save it for what? Perhaps to alert someone, if anyone got within hearing distance?

"I've got an idea I'd like to try in the morning," he said. "There are plenty of fish in that river. Are you very attached to your apron?"

Now she was sure she was the one wearing a look of confusion. What did the two have to do with each other?

He looked slightly chagrined in the flickering firelight. "I was thinking if I cut thin strips from the ties, I could make a fishing line. Maybe carve a quick fishhook."

Fish for breakfast.

Her stomach made an audible agreement. She reached behind her to untie the apron.

There was something intimate about removing the simple outer garment. When her gaze flicked up to his, she saw his stare skitter away.

"Here." She extended it to him.

He took it from her with a nod of thanks. "I'll try to leave it so it can be repaired..."

"Maybe we can use it for a flag—surely there'll be someone to wave down tomorrow."

He nodded, but she felt a fissure of unease as his eyes traveled around their crude campsite.

What if no one came for them?

Three

HUNGER DROVE the man from where he slept fitfully on the ground between the fire and the woman's shelter. Before he left their rough camp, he stirred up the coals and added twigs and then two larger logs to the fire. He intended to bring back breakfast and the fish would taste better cooked.

He glimpsed the woman's face as he straightened from the fire, her features slack in sleep. Her beauty hit him all over again, trapping his breath in his chest.

Beautiful. He'd called her that last night. When he had, there'd been almost a... hesitation in the air between them. He didn't know what it meant.

He worked to keep his steps quiet among the decayed leaves underfoot, avoided twigs that would crack under his boots. Out in the open, the ground was dry and parched, with cracks snaking through the yellowing grass. How long had it been since it had rained?

At the river's edge, he slipped a shaking hand into his pocket to remove the slender wooden fishhook he'd whittled last night by the fire. He'd carefully separated a narrow strip of fabric from the woman's apron. He'd taken two strips and knotted them together to make it twice as long. Now he affixed the hook onto the end with a strong knot.

He was keenly aware that his body, and the woman's too, were in desperate need of sustenance. Still weak after being sick, after the energy lost from swimming in the river, surviving the rapids and cold water.

An echo of gnawing hunger swamped him. Not from his body right now, but something from the past. He forced the feeling back, walking in the growing morning sunlight until he found just the spot he wanted—a bend in the river that made for a deeper pool of slow water and sheltered by the roots of a tree that had grown up on the bank, only to find the soil beneath it slowly being washed away.

That's where the man dropped his hook.

There should be bait on his hook, sense told him. But he had none.

He waited, the apron-string line tugging against the gentle flow of water. Eventually he became aware of movement farther down the bank, then the swish of the woman's dress against the tall grasses as she approached slowly.

Sunlight glinted off the water, sending golden beams skittering across her skin. He felt a pull inside, almost enough to draw him toward her. Only the feel of the line in his hands, the hunger in his belly, kept him where he was.

Something tugged on the line.

The man's eyes flicked to the water, to the new tension on the line as it disappeared into the depths.

Another tug.

This time he yanked back, felt the weight of something thrashing on the other end of the makeshift fishing line.

He pulled in the string, hand over hand, and at the last, flipped a shimmering green and brown fish onto the bank.

It kicked and flopped, but he quickly captured it in his hands. Instinct had him hold it by the lip, squeezing tightly with his thumb as he disengaged the hook from the fish's mouth.

She joined him on the bank, squatting next to him, the fish between them.

"Here's our breakfast." He breathed the words. Felt satisfaction and another beat of urgency flow at the same time. It wasn't enough, the fish too small to feed both of them.

They needed more.

The woman's eyes sparkled like the sunlight on water. "May I try?"

H secured the fish, weighting it down with a partial log.

Her first attempt at tossing the hook and line into the water splashed wide with a *ploop!* and she looked to him for help. He came behind her, close enough that his nose could press into her hair if he leaned forward the slightest bit.

"Here. Like this." His right hand closed gently over her wrist and he guided her toss so that the hook dropped in the water at just the right spot.

Her head tilted, and he caught the flash of white teeth in her smile. A wisp of her hair caught in the scruff at his jaw, and he had to force himself to concentrate.

Fishing.

Food.

Survival.

"Keep a bit of tension in the line," he told her quietly.

Her head turned—so slightly—as if she felt the brush of his words on her cheek. But she didn't shy away. From him or his touch. Whatever distrust she'd held for him yesterday, it seemed to have gone with the rising of the sun.

A new noise came to him over the sound of the burbling river.

She was humming.

She did that a lot.

He couldn't say how he knew, only that he did.

A flash of the sketches in the notebook popped into his mind. There'd been a small bird on several pages, in a corner or along the inside margin.

A song sparrow.

Some tenuous connection to her clicked into place. *Sparrow*.

It wasn't a name, but somehow it fit.

Light filtered through the leaves, creating patterns on the ground around them. Something stirred inside his mind.

"I remember fishing," he murmured. She didn't look at him, but he had the sense that she was listening.

He was conscious of what had happened yesterday when he'd tried to grasp on to the memory. This time, he let the images float there in his mind, not pushing. Not chasing after them.

"Not exactly like this," he said the words barely above a whisper. "We had... poles, I think."

His memories painted images of soft light and trees, leaves, a little creek. The scent of mud, brown and rich and fragrant with decay came strongly, a visceral memory.

"By yourself?" Her whisper barely registered.

"No." Childish laughter rang in his head. "With my brother. And my father."

He could see his father's serious expression. Pa was always serious. The memory brought on a tender feeling of affection that was all-encompassing. The knowledge settled somewhere deep inside the man. Pa. And Peter.

"We must've fished for hours," he told her. "Until the sun began to go down and our damp clothes became unbearable."

"My father taught me to clean a fish." The memory settled over him as he told it. His pa's scarred hands, patient explanation. The knowledge of what he must do to get their breakfast ready. "I can still remember the taste of it, breaded and coming out of that frying pan on our old stove."

His tongue almost felt singed anew with the memory of the hot, buttery goodness.

His stomach rumbled loudly, breaking him out of the hazy thoughts. They drifted away like dander on a fierce spring breeze and he felt the loss keenly.

"My father was a good teacher," he recalled. He felt the love and security of those moments in his memory.

"You must be just like him," she murmured.

He blinked at her words, then noticed the tension ratchet up in the end of her line.

"Pull now." He reached for her, but she had already tugged the wriggly fish up onto the bank.

She squealed a bit, danced as it flopped toward her feet.

A laugh escaped him. It sounded rusty. Why did it sound like that?

He scooped up the fish before it could flop back into the water. "Good work."

Her eyes were warm, and for a moment, another memory flashed. A woman in a beautiful pale pink dress, flowers clutched against her midsection. A feeling of love so overwhelming that he caught his breath in the present moment.

One blink and the memory was gone, so quickly that he realized he hadn't seen the woman's face.

A wedding. His wedding. He was sure of it.

A strong, protective urge rose up inside of him. If Sparrow was his wife, he must do everything he could to keep her safe.

Up until this moment, there'd been a vague feeling of partnership with her in this strange world he'd woken up in —a world of no memories. Something had broken free along with the memory of his pa.

But this new feeling was different. A threat.

Run!

The shifting currents beneath the water, the rustling in the grass, the shadows amongst the woods. All of them seemed menacing.

He'd told her yesterday that staying in place would mean their best chance of being found, being rescued, but was that true? They'd had success fishing this morning, but what if tomorrow the fish didn't bite?

Clouds drifted together on the far horizon, pushed by the brisk breeze. For a fraction of a second, a thought skittered through his mind that a storm was coming.

He couldn't know that.

But the sense of unease didn't lift.

Ten lost.

Ten days lost?

Was it eleven now? Or twelve, or maybe even thirteen?

He didn't know how much time had been taken by the sickness and memory loss that plagued them. What if the help he hoped was coming, didn't exist?

Ten days lost in the wilderness was far too many. If no one was looking for them, he was putting both of them in danger by insisting they stay put.

He couldn't look at her as she tossed the hook back into the water, as he knelt over the two fish with his pocketknife, thankful that soon the hunger pangs in his belly would be satisfied.

What was the right decision? He wished he knew.

The woman sat back from the campfire, warm and full. She licked the grease of the fish from her fingers. H had threaded them onto a slender stick and cooked them over the fire.

She should've been embarrassed at how she'd devoured it before it had even cooled—like she was a wild animal. Or half-starved, which was more accurate.

That had been hours ago. Even though they'd had fish for breakfast too, she'd never been more happy to eat the same food for two meals in a row.

H sat across the fire, staring into the flames as if deep in thought. She had a passing feeling that this wasn't the first time she'd seen him pensive.

After breakfast, he'd left their camp to go scouting while she'd stayed behind. His departure had unsettled her. The quietness had seemed threatening without him near, so she'd busied herself with hunting for more sticks and branches to feed the fire.

He'd raised one eyebrow when he'd returned to camp, but before a defensive word could escape her lips, he'd smiled. Asked whether she'd hummed the entire time she'd gathered wood.

She hadn't known how to answer that. She'd noticed the songs from inside her, though most of the words still eluded her. The humming had begun unconsciously.

Now the warmth of the fire and the sun overhead made her feel almost drowsy. She roused herself when she felt her head bob with sleep. Sat up straighter. Caught the grin twitching his lips.

But when he spoke, he was serious. "You should nap," he said. "It's difficult to sleep through the night on the hard ground. And we may need to leave our camp behind in the morning."

Leave camp?

"Why?" She didn't mean for the word to emerge breathless and weak.

He glanced to the side, briefly giving her his profile. A muscle ticked in his jaw. "I've been thinking on it all morning. We've only got this crude shelter. No blankets. No tools. It's dangerous for us to stay here."

How could that be? She'd learned the crude path to the river. Recognized the shape of the trees as she'd searched the woods for downed trees and branches for their fire. She'd begun to feel safe as the surrounding area had become more familiar.

He seemed to read the direction of her thoughts. His eyes made a circuit of their surroundings, too.

"There's a rugged beauty to it, isn't there?" he asked gently. "A wildness that calls to me." He paused. "But what if it storms? Your shelter isn't waterproof."

And he hadn't slept under any shelter at all, last night.

"What if a wild animal approaches?"

She resisted the urge to remind him of the gun at his hip. He'd told her yesterday that he had only the bullets inside it. There were no more once the ammunition ran out.

"What if someone comes looking for us?" she asked. Her eyes roved the small shelter, the fire, the broken branches just beyond H.

"There's been no sign of anyone today. It would help if we could remember how many days since we've been out here."

"You remembered something this morning." Her argument only made him shift his legs, extending one long leg parallel to the fire.

"Not anything helpful to us."

Was it her imagination, or did he seem cagey as he answered, his gaze flitting to the side.

"Our memories may come back." She'd held onto that thought since she'd woken this morning.

"What if they don't?" he asked. "What if the fish aren't biting tomorrow?"

She could still feel the echoes of the roaring hunger, a hunger so deep she'd felt it in her bones. She didn't want to starve out here.

"And we've no medicine," he said. "The thing that frightens me most is imagining us eating something and getting bad sick again—or getting cut and having an infection."

He was right.

She knew he was right.

But some visceral need deep inside said not to leave the

safety of what she knew. She knew this place now. Knew how to survive in the most basic sense, even if H had brought up that the fish, their source of food, might not be there forever.

"We'll go together," he said. "We can craft a torch, take the fire with us."

But they didn't even know where they were going.

She breathed in deeply as panic tried to swamp her. "I don't want to go," she admitted. "I'm afraid."

The words shook something loose inside her mind. A memory that flashed quickly. A woman's—her mam's?—face, a flash of a smile meant to reassure, but the worried eyes expressed everything.

"We must keep our chins up," the memory Mam said. The arm she put around the little girl's shoulder felt so real, as if she could feel it right now. "I've learned to make the best of every circumstance, and so must you."

The memory danced away, leaving the woman shaken by the feeling of familiar warmth, the scent of baking bread.

"What's the matter?" H asked. He'd shifted to his haunches and edged around the fire. He stopped within touching distance, hands on his knees. One hand had risen, as if he was reaching for her, but he hesitated.

The woman wiped one hand over her cheek, surprised when it came away dry after the bout of emotion in the memory. "I think I remembered something, too."

She didn't think about it, didn't pause, just reached out and grabbed his hand. His longer fingers closed over her smaller ones, warmth from his skin enveloping her. For a moment, she felt a swoop in her stomach, like swinging too high.

At certain moments, H seemed so familiar to her. He'd reached for her, and she'd done what had felt right. But something about this connection, the intimacy of holding hands, seemed completely new, foreign.

And yet, still right.

His gaze held hers. She felt as if she could read the same feelings in his eyes.

"What did you remember?" he prompted.

She shook her head, breaking their gaze and somehow thankful for the relief of it. "Nothing helpful. A moment with... I think, my mam. Telling me that I must learn to make the best of my circumstances." With her free hand, she rubbed the sudden ache in her forehead just above the bridge of her nose. "I can't even remember what happened to prompt the words."

His big hand squeezed hers gently. "Sound advice."

"But?"

He shook his head slightly. "We still can't stay here."

Everything he said made logical sense. She was the one out of step.

The knot of fear in her belly tightened. "What if we could help get ourselves found?"

His gaze questioned her.

"What if we took our fire out in the open," she suggested. Her words came faster as the thoughts tumbled into place. "And built it as big as we can—use every piece of wood we find."

"Create a tower of smoke," he finished. He let go of her hand to rub his hand at his jaw, considering.

Her heart flew around in her chest. If there were others looking for her and H, the smoke could signal their location.

"It's a brilliant idea, Sparrow."

She wrinkled her brows.

He looked slightly chagrined as he admitted, "Ever since I heard you humming this morning, I've been calling you that in my head."

Sparrow.

A sparrow sang outside the tiny childhood bedroom she'd shared with her mam and brother, its beautiful trill coming just before dawn every morning. The knowledge emerged inside her, right and true.

"If you mind the nickname, I won't—"

"I don't mind." Suddenly shy, she couldn't quite look at him as she pushed up to stand.

He followed, and she realized, not for the first time, how tall and broad he was.

"I'll scout out a place on the riverbank where we can put your bonfire," he said.

She nodded without looking at him. "I'll start gathering more wood."

"You shouldn't wear yourself out," he warned. "If no one comes looking for us, we should still plan to leave in the morning."

Her heart sank. If someone did come, it would change things. Whoever might be looking for them surely knew their names, their identities.

But she and H wouldn't stay in this little clearing, no matter what happened.

The knot in her stomach remained. The future was unclear, and she didn't like it.

* * *

"You'll want to apply the salve in the morning and before you go to bed at night."

Doc Goodwin hovered just outside the tent, listening to the advice delivered in sweet tones. He'd been with this particular company for nearly a week—a transplant after leaving an eastbound wagon train that had suffered from bad leadership—and had yet to see one patient.

All because of the young lady inside that tent.

"Thank you, Miss Maddie," an older, feminine voice said.

The tent flap was thrown back and what must be Miss Maddie emerged.

She was looking down, maybe at the wicker basket she held over one arm, and didn't see him. The tent flap came down behind her, and despite his best intentions to see inside, he didn't get a glimpse of the patient.

He followed her for a few feet before irritation had him spewing, "Excuse me."

She stopped, but was rifling through her basket and didn't look up. Around them, Tremblay's camp was quiet. No one seemed to know what to do without their wagon master or clear directives from the captains.

Doc took a step closer. "I've been hoping to meet you," he said. "I understand you've—"

She finally looked up, her bonnet slipping back so that he had a clear view of her face.

She was younger than he'd thought—much younger than his thirty-six years. Her unlined face and guileless eyes put her age anywhere from nineteen to twenty-one.

But it was her beauty that hit him like a blow to the kidney. The spray of freckles across her pert nose, the intelligence in her blue eyes framed with sooty lashes that could tease or flirt. Beneath the bonnet, hair the color of fire. Strands had come loose somewhere along the way and framed a graceful jaw.

His breath lodged in his chest. One blink and shame flowed through him, hot and slow like a river of lava he'd once read about in a geology textbook. His lips firmed in disdain at himself, even as he saw the flicker of recognition and the minute narrowing of her eyes.

He cleared his throat, blamed a night of tossing and turning in his bedroll for the discombobulation. "I'm Dr. Jason Goodwin. Folks call me Doc. I thought it was time we met."

Jason.

What had possessed him to introduce himself that way? It was easier to think of himself as Doc, to lean into his occupation. His late wife, Marie, had been the only one who used his given name. Jason was gone. The same way she was.

The young woman's smile, when it came, was tight. "Maddie Fairfax."

She stuck out her hand and it took a beat too long for his sluggish brain to realize she meant to shake his hand like a man might.

A flush rose high on his cheeks as his hand enveloped hers. The slight feel of her fingers in his, the brush of her palm. It was too much. He dropped her hand like a burning coal.

Resisting the urge to clear his throat again—was he having an allergic reaction to the pollen of some nearby plant?—he jerked his thumb toward the tent she'd only just vacated. "Perhaps I should examine the patient."

"Why?" Her expression showed nothing more than simple curiosity, but he heard wary tones in her voice.

"I've heard good reports about how helpful you've been to the company thus far..."

She didn't smile. Simply waited.

"But I'm a doctor by profession."

Her eyes cut to the tent and back to him. When she sidled closer, he found himself holding his breath.

"Mrs. Barrigan asked for me." She said the words with a smile that was somehow void of warmth. "As you said, I've formed a rapport with the travelers in this company. They know me."

She threw out the last words like a challenge. Her eyes flashed and her chin came up. Something in his gut twisted in response.

"And where did you gain your medical degree?" Now his words threw a gauntlet. "A woman's college? Apprenticing with a professional doctor?"

The flicker of unease passed behind her eyes.

"Ah. You don't have one." He kept his tone matter-of-fact. "I'm sure you mean well, Miss, but I've seen firsthand how home remedies and old wives tales can do more harm than good. The trail itself is dangerous enough."

He saw the protest rise to her lips and jumped in before she could give it voice. "Mrs. Mason almost died from an infection," he told her. "She would've died had it not been for my medicine." He patted the black bag in his left hand.

It was true. God knew how close it had been, the number of prayers Doc and Owen, Rachel's husband, had sent heavenward. It had been a near thing.

Rachel was fully recovered now, and Doc had joined this

westbound train. Two hundred and twelve souls. Several of the women were carrying babies in their wombs. Doc was needed here, along with his real medicine, not herbs.

"Miss Maddie, Miss Maddie!"

She turned away first, but Doc was right on her heels as a boy no older than ten reached them. He bent over, hands on his knees, as he tried to catch his breath.

Maddie knelt at his side, one hand going to his shoulder. "What's the matter?"

"Tommy's stitches came loose."

Tears streamed down the boy's cheeks as the words tumbled out. He wiped his face with one grubby hand, smearing dirt through the tears.

Doc went on alert. Opened stitches meant an open wound. If infection set in, it could be deadly. "Where is this patient?" Doc asked.

The boy sniffled and glanced from Maddie to Doc.

"It's all right, Alex," she said.

Doc had to look away from where her hand soothed the boy.

"He's in our wagon." Alex pointed across the clearing. "Miss Maddie, ya gotta stitch him back up."

Doc stepped closer and bent to speak to the boy. "I think it would be prudent if I went with you and put in the stitches."

Alex looked tearfully at him, suspicion evident. "Who're you?"

"This is Doc," Maddie said gently. "He's got a fancy medical degree from back East."

He bristled. She didn't have to put it that way.

He found his smile turning into more of a grimace.

"I've performed countless surgeries and assisted in many more. I'm certain I can put in stitches that will stay closed for your patient."

He caught Maddie's narrowed eyes as she stood up and motioned Doc across the clearing. "By all means."

The boy still looked between them, though his eyes had taken on a new shine. "You're a real doctor?"

He heard the quiet exhale but didn't glance at Maddie. "I am."

"C'mon!"

Doc followed the boy at a jog that got his heart pumping. This was why he'd joined this wagon train—and the one before it. People needed him. Doing good works was the only thing that helped erase the grief. Otherwise, it threatened to overwhelm him.

He was conscious of Maddie trailing behind. He spoke over his shoulder, though he didn't let himself look at her. "I'm certain I won't need assistance."

But she followed them anyway.

Alex climbed into the wagon, throwing out, "You better wait there. Ma doesn't like anyone tracking mud in our wagon."

Doc started to protest, but Maddie stayed him with a hand on his forearm.

Her touch burned like a brand and he jerked away from her. "If you please."

He saw what might've been a flash of hurt before her expression blanked.

The wagon jostled. It was easier to slip into his bedside persona than to think about the slight girl at his side. He set his bag on the ground and opened it, pulling out his fine suture needle. He had his catgut in hand when Alex edged out of the wagon and dropped to the ground with a small brown dog in his arms.

The boy's eyes were hopeful as he presented the squirming ball of fur to Doc. "This is Tommy. He don't like strangers much."

The little dog growled at Doc, baring its teeth.

"This." A breath. "Is Tommy?"

He could see Maddie from the corner of his vision. She seemed to be biting her bottom lip. To keep a smile from blooming?

She could've warned him.

Alex continued waiting with that hopeful look on his face. He held the dog securely and presented one front paw, where a gash stood out on the dog's forearm. The fur had been shaved away and clean black stitches were visible, at least where they hadn't been torn out by doggy teeth.

"Would you like me to take over for you?" Maddie asked sweetly. "I'm sure such a prestigious doctor such as yourself has other important tasks to look after."

Anger stirred at her trickery. She'd been making a fool of him all along. But Doc was conscious of the boy watching him. He'd been a boy once, with a dog that had followed him around day and night, slept at the end of his bed.

Doc shook his head. He wouldn't let her win. "I'll be happy to stitch him up."

He had needle and thread in hand so he carefully closed up the wound with finger and thumb, avoiding those canine teeth. He couldn't help but examine the stitches still intact.

"Miss Maddie does fine stitching, don't she?" Alex asked.

"They are good sutures," he said reluctantly.

But when he glanced up, Maddie was already gone.

51

Four

IT HADN'T WORKED.

Sparrow lay huddled in the tree shelter, staring out into the night.

She had spent the entire afternoon ranging farther and farther away from the campsite, finding every downed log, branch, twig, and piece of tree bark she could find and delivering them to H, who had fed them to a bonfire that stretched ten feet in the sky and sent a plume of dark smoke heavenward. Her skin and hair still smelled like smoke, even now.

As the afternoon had waned into the evening, she'd returned to the fire with another armful of wood. With every load, H's shoulders drooped more.

When the sun slipped behind the horizon, he'd told her no more. No more wood. They would let the fire burn out.

That had been hours ago.

Thunder rumbled from the clouds gathering on the horizon behind her. She didn't understand how it could rain when the cold air felt so dry. Or maybe the storm was far away. She huddled deeper beneath the fragrant cedar boughs H had cut with his knife.

She'd seen the nicks in his hands, the scraped knuckles. A pocketknife wasn't the right tool to cut away the branches and boughs, but he'd done it anyway. And it was a good thing, because this cool air had pushed through as their bonfire had winked out.

Even with the extra insulation of the branches, she couldn't seem to get warm. She shivered beneath the shelter, hugging herself, while H lay near the fire. In the dim, flickering light, she saw his body quivering, too.

Was he asleep? It had been dark for a long time, but she'd been unable to quiet her mind. Thoughts of the unknown, what they might face tomorrow, kept her from sleep, even though her body was exhausted.

When another rumble of thunder broke the silence, she shifted beneath the branches. H's head turned slightly.

Awake, then.

She slipped from beneath the scratchy branches. He caught her movement and sat up. As she drew closer, the flickering firelight highlighted the lines of concern around his eyes.

"Can't sleep?" he asked.

She shook her head.

He looked surprised for the barest moment when she folded her legs beneath her and sank to the ground beside him.

The fire popped, the scent comforting. But the warmth only extended to the tip of her nose and brushed her cheeks.

She couldn't stop shivering.

But when he unbuttoned his slicker and opened it as if he was going to take it off, she shook her head. He couldn't be any warmer than she was. It wasn't a winter coat.

Instead of taking it off, he extended his arm. When she leaned closer, he tugged her into the curve of his body, letting the coat enclose as much of her as it could.

Heat from his body seared her as she nestled into him. His arm was a comforting weight over her shoulders and she let her cheek rest against his chest. After those first few hours, her wariness had seeped away.

It seemed... natural to trust him. He was protective, he watched over her. He constantly scanned the horizon and had warned her about the berries.

H had made her feel safe.

His chest rose and fell, his hand flexed against her elbow. Some tension eased out of him. Had he been worried about her? Or was he soaking in the warmth of sitting close like this, too?

Another low rumble of thunder. This one quieter. Farther away? Today as she'd ranged farther and farther afield in search of firewood, she'd seen the cracked ground, all the summer grasses dead or dying.

H had been right when he'd said earlier this afternoon that if it rained, her shelter wouldn't provide much cover. The fire would be doused in a strong rain, though it seemed less and less likely that they would see any moisture tonight.

"We can't stay here," she murmured.

"No, we can't." His chest rumbled beneath her ear.

There was no use wishing someone had come for them today. There was only the fear of the unknown, not knowing what would happen tomorrow. What if they never found anyone? What if they walked into danger?

Or what if they searched for help in the completely wrong direction?

He must've felt her rising tension as questions and worries swirled, but he didn't try to comfort her with platitudes. His hand rubbed up and down her arm, sending goosebumps skittering down her spine. Then he clasped his hand over her elbow, a steady weight that was more comforting than any words.

"Where do you think we are?" she whispered.

She'd seen him flipping through the small, leather-bound book as he'd tended the bonfire.

"Nebraska Territory, maybe. Or Utah Territory. Near as I can figure it from these notes, at least. And that's if I calculated the miles up correctly."

They truly were in the wilderness. Miles from civilization.

"It's possible we were part of a wagon train. The notes in this book seem to indicate stopping places to allow animals to graze."

But she heard what he didn't say. If they had traveled with a wagon train, how had they ended up out here alone?

"We'll follow the river," he said. "If there are other travelers, they'll want water for their livestock."

The fire flickered, casting shadows against the trees across the clearing.

"While you were hunting firewood, I caught some more fish. Put them on a makeshift stringer down in the water. We'll have food until we find the next place to camp."

"Clever."

His chest expanded beneath her at her faint praise.

"We'll be all right," he said.

But was there a way to be sure of it?

He must have sensed her doubt, because he rested his jaw atop her head.

This was the closest they'd been physically. It felt necessary, because of the chilly air. She was certainly warmer, tucked against him like this, than she'd been under a blanket of boughs. And he seemed to have no reservations about having her close.

"Do you... do you really think we're married?" she whispered.

They must be. Surely they must be in order to end up together out here in the wild. A stranger wouldn't have been swept into the river with her, would he? Had their wagon been lost? Their belongings? Questions swirled.

He didn't shift away, but she felt the stillness in him.

"I had another memory," he said softly. "Only a partial one. A fancy dress, like someone would wear at a wedding. A clutch of flowers. It felt... real."

A knot in her belly loosened and butterflies took flight. She was married to H. Somehow, it felt right.

The awareness had crackled between them all day. It was there when he glanced up as she dumped her load of sticks and twigs. The cut of her eyes to him, the way she couldn't ignore where he was as she'd readied for bed and climbed into the shelter.

It was a relief, somehow, to acknowledge it.

Her heart took flight as she tipped her head toward him. He shifted slightly and lifted his head. Now they were face to face. His hand clasped her shoulder.

She reached up to touch his jaw. The stubble scratched

her sensitive palm. His dark eyes appraised her, waiting patiently for her next movement.

"How can it be possible that I don't recognize this face," she whispered. "But that my heart recognizes yours?"

Her fingertips grazed his cheek, his temple. He closed his eyes as she ran her fingers down the bridge of his nose, then gently past his lips to his chin. His eyes flashed open and he let loose a low groan, as if he couldn't hold it in any longer. His hand moved from her shoulder to cup her jaw, and he leaned forward.

"Tell me if you don't want this," he whispered fiercely.

Her only answer was to tip her face up so her lips brushed his.

That gentle, barely-there touch wasn't enough. For either of them.

His hand slipped to the back of her neck, fingers tunneling into her hair, to tug her closer. His lips slanted over hers, warm and tender.

Maybe it was the fear uncoiling inside her, that his embrace felt like a safe place to hide, but she leaned into his claiming kiss.

It felt as if the first time she'd experienced such a kiss. It must be because of the memory loss, it had to be, if they were married. And yet this felt like the very first kiss. Like anticipation—had he been thinking about her all day? The way she had been thinking about him?

Like hope.

Like home.

A loud pop from the fire and he pulled back reluctantly. His eyes roamed her face as he tucked a dislodged tress of hair behind her ear from where it had fallen in her eyes.

His tender touch brought on a haze of tears.

"Hey. It's all right," he whispered.

He brushed a kiss to the center of her forehead and then shifted, tucking his coat around her again, pulling her into his side. "You should rest. We don't know what kind of terrain we'll meet tomorrow."

His cautionary words made it hard for her to relax, but eventually she nodded off with her head against his shoulder.

* * *

H's heart pounded against his ribcage as Sparrow settled against him. Had she felt his hand shaking as he'd tucked that piece of hair behind her ear?

He was grateful for the chance to turn his face to the fire as her head tucked between his neck and shoulder. He couldn't explain the emotion that had come over him as his lips had found hers. It wasn't only a strong, protective urge that had risen inside him but a tender affection, and something else. There was a strangeness about her lips under his. It felt bone deep, as if the familiarity he'd felt all day didn't extend to the kiss, to having her in his arms.

It must be the poison from the berries affecting him. He'd seen the wedding in his memories. Sparrow must be his wife.

But for those moments after the kiss, when she'd looked at him with such trust in her eyes, he'd felt panic rising up inside him. He couldn't explain why. Or how it was more than being stranded in the wilderness, alone, with no tools and limited ammunition. It was her. An uncertainty about the kiss they'd shared.

He shouldn't dwell on it. The feeling was already receding. It would do little good for him to try and suss out its origins, not without his memory.

Sparrow's breaths evened out, and she leaned more heavily against him. He'd fed the fire a big log not long ago, and it would burn consistently for a while yet.

Uncertainty swamped him even as this sign of her trust, that she'd sleep tucked against him, should've been reassuring. It was far from the distrust of yesterday.

What if traveling upriver was a mistake?

He'd hoped vainly that her idea of sending up a tower of smoke would attract help. He'd spent part of the afternoon hiking downstream, not expecting to find people but needing to eliminate the possibility.

Not far from the river, there'd been signs of wagons crossing, ruts in the grass as if it had been merely days since conveyances had traveled in this direction. There'd been numerous old campfires, stamped out. A lone sock left behind in the grass.

Signs of the wagon train should've been comforting, but if they'd crossed this terrain, why hadn't they come looking for H and Sparrow?

Was there something more sinister at play? Was it possible they'd been exiled from a caravan? Or perhaps everyone had succumbed to a sickness and they'd been the only survivors. But then where were their supplies?

Or could his log book mean that he was a scout, that he and his companion had traveled farther afield than they'd intended? What if the caravan had left without them?

A large caravan like the one he'd seen signs of wouldn't travel quickly. Most of the pioneers would walk while oxen carted the heavy wagons loaded with supplies.

How did he know that? He felt it with such certainty. He *must* have been traveling on one of those wagon trains.

Even so, if H and Sparrow had been left behind for days, it might not be possible for them to catch up on foot.

H should've had a horse. It didn't make sense that he was on foot.

Sparrow's breath caught and she jerked. Her head tipped from where it rested against his shoulder and she came fully awake.

"All right?" he asked.

From the corner of his eye, he saw her blinking rapidly, saw awareness slip back into her expression.

"I dreamed—but I don't think it was a dream. I think that was a memory," she said quickly. "I saw part of it this morning, or rather felt it." She exhaled noisily, rubbed one hand over her face as if to clear away cobwebs that remained.

"Do you want to tell me about it?"

"It feels so tenuous," she said. "There's a woman—my mam." She shook her head slightly, her arm bumping against his. "I think she's... packing." Her voice pitched quieter. "She lost her job. As a... cook, I think? There's something... I can't—something bad happened. We had to move." Her voice grew stronger. Maybe the memory had solidified? "Everything I'd known, all my friends, had to be left behind. She must've felt the same fears. Where would we go? My brother and I would need provided for."

A faint sadness tinged her words. "She didn't show any fear. I couldn't stop crying."

He could hear in her voice how the loss of that security had affected her. "That must've been difficult."

His arm had gone numb from where it'd been braced

behind her. He hadn't noticed it until she'd moved, until the rushing blood sent prickles of pain underneath his skin. When he could feel his fingers again, he let his hand close over hers on her knee. "Can you remember anything past those moments?"

She shook her head slowly. "Only her face. She was smiling, but her smile was hiding something. Her worry, maybe. Or uncertainty."

He squeezed her hand. "Those worries—food and shelter—are for a parent, not for the child you were."

She managed a small smile, but her brow remained wrinkled. "I think that's what she was trying to tell me."

"A man's heart deviseth his way: but the Lord directeth his steps."

Her smile turned wry at the verse from Proverbs. "We must've been okay." She rubbed her forehead. "I think so. I wish I could remember."

"Me too." If he knew what direction they should walk tomorrow, he'd feel more confident.

He shifted his legs, realizing that his left foot was falling asleep, too.

She seemed to notice his discomfort for the first time since coming awake. "I don't think either of us will get much sleep sitting next to the fire like this."

She glanced over her shoulder to the shelter. "It was too cold to sleep, even with the branches."

He shook his head to show his confusion. He didn't know what she was suggesting.

If he wasn't mistaken, a faint blush tipped her cheeks as she murmured, "We could lie down next to each other in the shelter, beneath the boughs. It would be warmer."

An instant denial sprang to his lips, but he swallowed

it. He could see the lines of exhaustion fanning from her eyes and the droop of her shoulders. It seemed they'd escape the threat of rainstorms—for now—as the thunder and clouds had moved away. But the chill that the far-off storm had brought wouldn't lift until the sun came up— and he planned to be long gone by then.

She was right. Their only hope of staying warm enough to sleep was to huddle together.

He followed her to the shelter and bumped against the upright branches, nearly dislodging one or two before he laid down at her side.

There wasn't enough room inside the small shelter for either of them to stretch out. She curled into him, her back to his front. He pulled several of the scratchy cedar boughs over them, turning his face away when one branch poked into his cheek.

It was awkward in the darkness. Without the fire near, he could only see the shadow of her. He couldn't make out any features, though his face was only inches from her cheek.

When a tiny shiver shook her, he had no choice but to wrap his arm around her middle. Almost instantly, she settled more closely into him. Warmth bloomed where they touched. Her head softened into his sternum and her breaths evened out. She must be exhausted.

He was, too, but he couldn't settle. There was something inside him that reacted strongly to being the man who'd provided warmth and shelter, the man she could lean on to find comfort and peace enough to sleep. But there was also an unease inside him, an echo of what he'd felt when he'd kissed her. Was it wrong to be close like this?

He didn't have an answer for that. Both of them were

making the best guesses they could as to who they were to each other, how they'd ended up out here, and what they should do next. Holding her felt both right and wrong at the same time. He didn't understand how that could be.

Her skin was warm and he couldn't seem to keep himself from pressing his nose into the softness behind her ear. She smelled like the river water he'd seen her splash on her face, and something more. Something uniquely her.

He searched through the darkness of his mind, reaching for the memory he'd seen for only a snatch of time. The pink gown. He didn't know a thing about women's dresses, but he could see the quality of the work. The fine stitches, the lace at the cuffs. This was a special dress. He willed the woman in his memory to turn around. He glimpsed the flowers in her hands, but something about her fingers bothered him. As he tried to focus on why, the memory shifted.

A feminine voice, too low to make out. But he recognized the worried tone. Sunshine falling at an angle through a dingy window. A house?

He grabbed for the memory, tried to reorient the view. Who was speaking? Where were they? What was through that window?

But as he grasped for it, the memory faded and disappeared.

He stared into the darkness, holding Sparrow. Why had they left a home like the one that had flashed through his memory? What had they left behind?

He had no answers, only a deep disquiet as he held her in the darkness and wrestled with the shadows in his mind until he finally fell asleep.

Five

SPARROW STOOD SLIGHTLY BEHIND H, huddled in his shadow as he peered through the gloom. A warm, dry wind gusted, blowing strands of her hair into her eyes.

The two of them had spent all day walking beside the river—although, was walking the correct word? They'd scrambled over boulders, pushed through reeds in a sandy, marshy area, and the last two hours had picked their way up a gravel incline to traverse this bit of riverbank where the water cut a deep ravine through the land.

"Do you smell smoke?" H asked now, voice barely above a whisper.

She shook her head. It was silly, because she stood behind him. When he prompted, "Sparrow?" she whispered, "No."

Her nose detected only dust and sweat and the peat-like scent that meant rain was coming. For the past hours, towering clouds had rolled in, obliterating the sky.

Thunder grumbled in the distance, but the air still felt too dry to mean rain.

She didn't feel much like a sparrow right now—or perhaps she did. Fear swirled inside her, beating like the wings of a bird. She wanted to shout, "Run away!" but something inside her snatched her voice.

H turned toward her. For one moment she was enveloped in his heat, safe in the protective circle of his arms. But he was only urging her back the way they'd come.

When they reached the bend, the river rolled fierce and rapid. She started to get on her hands and knees to scrabble downward. H caught her arm in his hand.

With one finger over his lips, he guided her around a narrow cut in the land she hadn't noticed before. From here, she was hidden from the deer track they'd been on, completely out of sight of whatever H had been watching.

Her nostrils twitched. The scent of smoke.

H pulled her close under his arm and spoke directly into her ear. His words felt hot against her sensitive skin and she stifled a shudder.

"I think someone's got a camp up there."

For a moment, her heart thrilled. Was someone looking for them?

But then realization dawned. H hadn't called out, hadn't approached this possible camp. Were they in danger?

"I want to get closer," he murmured. "Figure out if whoever is up there is friend or foe."

The wind flicked dust against her cheeks and into her eyes. She gripped his shirt. "Don't go up there."

He smoothed his fingers across her cheek. "I'm gonna skirt around to the higher ground on the other side of the camp. Couldn't see anyone moving, but that doesn't mean much from the vantage point we had."

This time the gust of wind brought a stronger smell of smoke. How big was the campfire? In the growing dark, she saw the worry in his eyes.

"Here." H shrugged out of his coat, his arm brushing against her in their closeness. He wrapped the garment around her.

It was so big that it swamped her. But it also brought the warmth of his body, his familiar scent—the smell she'd breathed in when she'd woken in his arms this morning, her nose pressed into his neck—enveloping her.

"Be careful," she breathed.

He pecked her lips with a brief kiss and then disappeared around the jagged rocky edge.

She glanced around. The roaring water only feet away made her tremble. She couldn't say whether it was from the present danger or a memory that wouldn't surface. All day, she'd been plagued with flashes of faces—she couldn't remember the names to go with the people—and a humming voice in her head. She guessed it was her mam.

A tree had grown up on the rocky ledge above the water's edge, and she wedged herself between it and the boulder that made up part of the rocky wall arching above her head.

It must've only been a minute or so, but she already wondered where H was. How soon before he returned?

Be careful. The words she'd said to H echoed in her mind and a memory surfaced with crystal clarity.

"Be careful." She handed a bundle of loose papers to her brother. Joseph.

A beat of relief pulsed through her. She'd remembered her brother's name.

"You'll write to me? Promise."

There was Joseph's rogue smile. A train whistle blew and another figure approached through the crowd on the platform steps.

H.

"It's time."

In this memory, H looked younger by a few years, his face missing some of its lines. And serious. If possible, even more than the grave expression he'd worn only moments ago before he'd left her.

"Promise you'll look after my brother?"

H turned an unsmiling gaze on her and nodded. "You have my word."

He'd thumped Joseph on the shoulder and they'd gone, disappearing into the crowd as they boarded the train.

Sparrow blinked and the memory receded. H had been friends with her brother. There was something about his manner... a sadness she didn't recognize.

Where had Joseph gone?

Lightning cracked, cutting through the sky in a jagged line. Before she could brace, or even breathe, it seemed as if the whole world was crashing with thunder.

That had been close.

Shaking, she flexed her hands on the tree. She was safe, wasn't she?

Her mind clung to the distraction of her most recent memory. Was it strange that the H in her memory had barely glanced at her? He hadn't kissed her goodbye, hadn't looked at her with the affection and warmth he'd shown the past two days.

Perhaps they'd become close later, a time after the memory had taken place. Maybe Joseph had connected them.

But she couldn't quite shake the uneasy feeling that had taken root in her gut remembering the shadows in the memory-H's eyes. What had hurt him?

Another flare of too-close lightning flashed. Another crash of thunder. She cried out, the sound swallowed up by the roaring wind. This time when the wind swirled, the scent of smoke made her eyes water.

Was the river rising? The waves over the rocks had white caps now. Perhaps it was raining upstream?

Her heart thudded loudly in her ears. H had tucked her into this outcropping for safety—but he surely hadn't thought about the storm affecting the river. An awful feeling that something was wrong rolled over her in waves. It had been too long since he'd gone.

Lightning struck again, illuminating a tree branch hurtling downstream. Her lungs protested the smoke, and she couldn't help coughing.

She couldn't wait here. Not now.

Urgency knotted her stomach as she stepped away from the tree to go back up the path, in the direction H had gone.

What if the camp was abandoned, but H couldn't find his way back to her?

What if he'd been injured?

Thoughts tumbled and spun as she ascended this rise. And the hazy smoke grew thicker. Her foot slipped and without something to hold onto, she fell to her hands and knees. She forced herself back to her feet. She coughed again, breathing hard. She needed a better viewpoint.

In the dark, she strained her eyes to see through the smoke. This was more than a campfire, more than the bonfire she and H had created yesterday. Where was he?

She could barely make out the thinning trees—was this where she and H had stopped as he'd watched the camp? Beyond, a glowing red lined the horizon.

Fire!

Lightning struck again, illuminating two dark shadows moving in a jagged, awful dance through the smoke.

Fighting. Struggling.

And then it was dark again.

Fear held her immobile. H had told her to wait—

She forced her feet to carry her up the embankment, though she had to scrabble for footing. "H! Fire!"

Thunder rolled again. Frightened, she crouched and covered her head with one arm.

A jagged streak of light split the sky and illuminated someone—not H—with arm raised over a bundle on the ground.

Was that H?

"No!" The rolling thunder stole her voice again.

And then a sound. *Pow!* Different than the thunder, sharper somehow.

A man's cry.

"H!"

* * *

H had left Sparrow behind that rocky outcropping and made his way silently through the woods and around behind the campsite—or what he thought was a campsite. He'd seen a glimpse of a small campfire, a bedroll. A bundle that might've been clothes or supplies. With each step, smoke had grown thicker and thicker until it had enveloped him, blocking his view.

The trees thinned out on this bluff so he crouched behind what little cover he'd found in a large rock shaped like a goose egg.

Growing light on the horizon drew his attention from the campsite and his stomach twisted.

The smoke and glow could only mean one thing. Wildfire.

He looked up to the sky. The boiling clouds promised rain, but none fell. Not yet.

His legs twitched with the urge to run back to Sparrow. *Run!*

But a noise stopped him. He strained his ears. Was that the blow of a horse? The sound was distant. Was someone on the approach?

Friend or foe?

Lightning flashed and for a moment, a haze of white blurred H's vision.

Just as his sight began to clear, a darker blur emerged from the smoke and struck out.

He ducked to the side, but he moved a second too slow. That moment of surprise meant he took the blow on his shoulder. When he would've pushed up and faced his attacker head-on, the man's—it had to be a man, tall and broad—foot came out and swept H's feet out from under him.

He sprawled in the dry undergrowth and rolled away

just in time to feel a kick that'd missed its target by a hairs-breadth.

"Who are you?" H demanded as he jumped to his feet.

Lightning split the sky again, revealing a craggy face. Dark pits where the man's eyes should be.

A ghost.

Or was the blowing smoke obscuring H's vision? Ghosts didn't exist, couldn't have knocked him down.

Dark again, thunder so deep it made it feel as if the ground was rolling beneath H's feet. He coughed, the sound jarring.

The man hadn't moved toward H. He was there, a shadow in the darkness. Listening? Why didn't he answer?

"My—I'm lost out here," he said urgently, stifling the urge to cough again. He'd almost mentioned his wife—Sparrow.

Something inside him had choked back the words before they emerged. If this person wasn't a friend, he didn't want him to know about Sparrow.

"Are you a scout?" H demanded, the man's silence threatening.

Another lightning strike illuminated the moment when the man turned—away.

No.

If the man was out here on horseback, he might've sighted a wagon train. Or fort. Somewhere H could find help. He threw himself at the retreating man, only for the man to whirl at the last minute and send a blow into H's midsection.

The unexpected pain brought tears to his eyes and stole his breath, the smoke making him gag. H gripped onto the man's coat, fingers sliding on leather. This wasn't a ghost. It was a flesh and blood man. Was the roaring crackle of the fire closer?

A glancing blow off H's ear caused a hiss of pain. And jolted a memory through him. Being struck across the head, jeering voices. Lying face down in the dirt, soil in his nose.

The fractured scene lasted only a second, but H's grip loosened and the man jerked away.

H got his hands up in front of him and blocked the neck blow thrown toward his face, but the man kicked out unexpectedly and connected with H's ankle.

He went down, fingers slipping against the pebbled ground, searching for purchase.

The man loomed over him, arm raised as lightning split the sky again. A few stray raindrops hit H's face. Instinct took over, and H drew his revolver from his holster, shooting at almost the same instant that the barrel cleared leather.

From the ground, he hadn't had the best angle. But when the man cried out, H knew his bullet had grazed him.

"H!" The wind muffled the cry, but H would know that voice anywhere.

Sparrow.

This time when the man darted away, H didn't follow.

His head was ringing as he dragged himself to his feet.

Sparrow appeared through a swirl of smoke.

It was so dark that he barely registered her wide, frightened eyes. She threw herself at him, and he held on with one arm, gun still drawn in his opposite hand.

His right shoulder ached where it'd been yanked. He twisted in a circle. The man wouldn't get the jump on him again. Not with Sparrow in the mix.

But all of H's instincts screamed that the man was gone.

Several heartbeats passed. He was slipping the gun back into its holster when far off lightning illuminated the sky enough to see Sparrow close.

Rain began to pelt them.

"Was there someone—?" she asked. When she pressed against him, he groaned, unable to keep the sound in when her body touched his tender, bruised ribs.

Her hand cupped his jaw. "I thought you'd been killed!"

Fear and anger surged. "I told you to stay put."

He began moving, anxious to get away. He heard hoofbeats over the sound of the rain, but he didn't want to be here if the man came back.

Foe.

H had gotten his answer.

Sparrow was talking. "...smoke... wildfire."

"The rain will douse it," he told her. Drops were sheeting down on them. Surely the wildfire wouldn't survive this torrent of rain.

"But the river is rising," she said.

For a moment, a memory surfaced. Him clinging to Sparrow's narrow waist beneath tumultuous water.

His anger that she hadn't listened to him ebbed completely in a wave of relief.

His hand closed around her waist. She was here, real and safe—for now—with him.

And only then did he realize that the driving rain wasn't soaking into the too-dry ground. Water rushed over his boots, over the ground. This rain could turn into a flash flood.

"We need to get somewhere safe."

It wouldn't be safe down low, near the river. And he didn't know which direction the man had gone.

In the dark, with water pouring from the sky in buckets, his sense of direction was discombobulated.

Or maybe it was his head.

A fierce pain felt as if his skull was splitting apart and he put one hand to his temple.

"H!"

He almost went to his knees, but some surge of protective instinct forced his numb feet to keep moving.

She tugged him by the arm when he couldn't see for the pain behind his eyes. Some of the rain abated and he forced his eyes open—when had he closed them?—to see she'd found a narrow opening where a bluff rose overhead. An alcove in the rock gave them some shelter.

Gave him some shelter. She'd pushed him to the inside and was still getting soaked.

It was dark, but he could make out the shape of her face. Her breath fogged at the open neck of his shirt.

She reached up to wipe his chin and he realized the warmth trickling from the corner of his mouth was blood.

"You're hurt." Her words held an accusing tone to them.

"He got the jump on me," H admitted. "But I'll be all right."

Her hand brushed against the left side of his ribcage. He couldn't hide the wince in these cramped quarters. He was close enough to see her face crumple.

He did what felt natural and gathered her to him, ignoring the twinge in his ribs. Somehow he knew his ribs were not broken, only bruised.

Sobs shook her slight body, so he nestled her even closer. They were both soaked through. Her skin felt chilled where her cheek pressed against his neck.

"Who-who was that?" she mumbled against his skin.

"I don't know. Not a friend."

Run! Even if the man hadn't been a scout looking for the two of them, the fact that he'd refused to help, to give any information, was a concern.

What was a man alone doing out here? Could he be some kind of mercenary? What was he looking for?

"We can't stay here. Need to keep moving," H said into her hair.

He'd put them in this danger, with his insistence that they search for help instead of waiting for it to come to them. He'd been the one to suggest staking out the campsite.

Now the man might decide to hunt the two of them.

H had put Sparrow in danger.

She shook her head, the movement brushing her nose back and forth across his skin.

"I'm fine," he murmured.

"I need to hold you for a moment more," she said.

His thoughts had been focused on the dangerous man, on their escape. But at her words, he registered the feel of her palms against the back of his neck, her fingers digging into his shoulders. The brush of her skirts against his legs. The feel of her back beneath his slicker and her dress.

This wasn't the moment for a kiss. Not when he'd struggled so mightily after their last kiss. Not when she was so upset. But he let himself cup the back of her head in his hand as she pressed close. Feel her alive in his arms, each shuddering breath something to be grateful for.

He couldn't seem to help edging her a half inch closer. He felt it too. Having someone care for him like she did—it felt like everything.

Like a home he'd been missing.

Like he'd do anything to protect her.

But what was he going to do now?

WITH A GROWING sense of danger and urgency, H pulled the two of them out of their alcove and into the rain before Sparrow was ready. Three steps out into the torrential downpour and water rushed over H's boots in rills down the incline. Suddenly, he felt an echo of the blow the man had landed on his ear.

For a moment, all he saw was an image of an older woman—his ma?—hurrying down a road at twilight, turning to send a tense smile over her shoulder at him. It only lasted for a second before his senses returned and he was back in the dark and pouring rain.

"Where are we going?" Sparrow asked.

H put one hand to his head, where slow beats of pain pulsed. "Away from here."

She was tucked up to his side and he felt her tip her head as if to look at him. "What's wrong? Did you get hit?"

"I'm fine for now."

But at that moment, another memory hit with the

force of a sucker punch straight to his gut and he stumbled over some protruding object on the ground.

Her hands steadied him, but he was bigger than her, heavier. He kept his feet, but barely.

"H!" The worry in her voice twisted his gut, but he soldiered on.

"We've got to put some distance between us and that man." H's words had a bit of a groan to them.

"We will. Just slow down."

He felt the heat of her palm against his stomach, through his sodden shirt. It was a point to anchor himself as memories swirled over him. He barely bit back a cry. Pressed his palm to his forehead.

"What is it?" Stark fear was audible in her voice.

"A memory—I think." He couldn't hold the words in, not with the moments battering him.

"My cousin Charles was my best friend. We did everything together. Sat at Ma's table to work on our reading after school. Worked in my pa's livery stable."

The rightness of the words slipped over him. He could remember the feel of Charles's arm slung over his shoulder, his teasing words as they'd walked home from school one afternoon. A fierce love rolled over H in a wave, strong enough to steal his breath.

Rain pelted his face and head but he didn't feel it. He barely registered Sparrow leading him through the darkness.

"We were... we were racing home after school one day. I can't—" He pushed back when his mind tried to steal the memory back into the darkness.

"There was something happening down the street." He saw the moments, as fractured as they must've been when he'd lived them. "Two men in a fight. A bad fight. One of them shot the other. I only had a glimpse because we were running. I was chasing Charles."

His chest began to ache as the memory unfolded further. The darkness and rain felt oppressive and foreboding.

Sparrow's arm squeezed his waist. "It's all right."

He shook his head, some dormant instinct firing. It wasn't all right. Never would be again.

"My back was turned. I don't know what happened after the gun was fired. The man who was shot tried to get on his horse, but the animal didn't like the scent of blood —that's what my pa said later. The horse bolted—"

And Charles had chosen that moment to dart across the street.

"Charles was run down." The words emerged hoarse. He was surprised they emerged at all. His throat felt like it was on fire. Grief swamped his chest.

"Did you see it happen?"

H wished for the oblivion he'd known moments ago. It was far, far better than this.

He'd been steps behind his cousin, calling out in glee because he was catching up. Unaware of the danger, of what he was about to cause.

"Someone bumped me." He remembered the feel of bodies around, disjointed now. "I would've been right behind him—might've been run over by the horse, too."

He'd been seconds too late.

"I held him," he whispered. "Someone was screaming— I don't know who."

Charles's eyes had already been glassy and empty when H had pulled his body into him. H had begged, had prayed, had screamed when someone had brought his pa and his uncle. When he'd been torn away from Charles's body.

He felt everything he'd experienced that day, all at once. Like being doused in the driving rain, only now it was emotion drowning him.

He didn't know what to do with it. Without warning, he lifted his face to the sky and cried, "aauugghh!"

Sparrow went still beside him, simply holding him.

Charles was gone.

And it was H's fault.

"It wasn't your fault," Sparrow whispered. Had he spoken aloud? He hadn't meant to.

More memories swirled around him, rolling over him like the river water bowling over rocks. His uncle, Charles's father, angry in their kitchen, spittle flying as he spoke to H's father. H watched from a hiding place behind the kitchen doorway. His uncle drowning his sorrow in a bottle behind the livery, where he was supposed to be working. He hadn't told a soul, only went into the livery to muck stalls.

His uncle had disappeared in the bottle, becoming angry and bitter. He'd left the livery, a business he and H's father had run together for years. Had cut ties with their family. H's actions had not only brought about Charles's death but separated his uncle from their family.

"You couldn't have known that the horse would bolt," Sparrow murmured.

When had he taken her in his arms? The rain was softening, moving off—or was it? And they stood holding each other in the dark.

He could hear the flooded river nearby. How close? Or

perhaps it was his pulse rushing in his ears, adrenaline fading as he'd lived through the terrible event all over again.

"I should've stopped him," H said. A burst of speed, a hand to pull Charles back.

"You were a child. It was a horrible accident."

But her words offered no real comfort. Her cheek pressed against his jaw, her arms tight about his shoulders. His rib ached where she leaned against him.

He couldn't accept her comfort. It wasn't right, not when he'd cost his family so dearly.

"We need to go." His words were jagged, rough. He pulled away from her body but kept her hand.

The darkness seemed to have grown—it wasn't the middle of the night yet, but no sliver of moonlight made it through the cloud cover or cut through the rain. They'd only taken a few steps when the muddy ground beneath his feet gave way and he stumbled.

He caught himself before he fell, but Sparrow stumbled too. She jerked in his grip. He kept her arm but heard her soft cry.

He steadied her, feeling the way the muddy ground, softer here, gave way beneath his boots. This was a dangerous place to traverse. In the dark, he couldn't see how close they were to the water.

"Are you all right?"

She moved slightly. Taking weight off her leg?

"My ankle—it twisted wrong when I took that step. But I think it's all right."

She took a tentative step. He couldn't see her, other than a dark shape in the darkness, but he heard the soft catch of her breath.

"I can keep go—"

He gripped her upper arm, only now catching the strength of her shivers. Her entire body shuddered with violent trembling. He tugged her into him, rubbing his hands up and down her arms.

"You're soaked through," he muttered. He'd been so caught up in his memories and grief that he hadn't registered even the most basic details about Sparrow.

"So are you."

He barely heard her words. What if he'd led them too close to the river's edge? In the darkness, it was impossible to see the terrain, and she'd gotten hurt because he hadn't been paying close enough attention.

Regret rose up in tandem with a protectiveness so fierce that it almost choked him.

"We can't light a fire, not with things this wet." He couldn't help himself. He brushed a kiss on the crown of her head. "But maybe we can find somewhere to keep the rain off."

"It doesn't feel like there's one dry inch on the earth," she said. Somehow, he heard the hint of humor in her voice. "I think we forgot to build our ark."

Her lightness tightened the cinch in his chest. He took a jagged breath.

"I'm all right to walk," she said evenly.

"I'd rather not walk into danger," he returned. "Surely there's somewhere near for us to hole up until morning."

He heard her soft noise of agreement.

But what would they do in the morning? He'd used one of his bullets. He didn't know whether the man who'd attacked him would track them, would attack again. Would he seek revenge because H's shot had connected? What if he was leading Sparrow into more and more danger?

Whatever hope he'd had to find a wagon train or a house out here was dwindling.

* * *

Sparrow was awake as the sky began to lighten.

It wasn't that the sun came up—the sky was still covered in slate gray clouds—but small details began to come into focus. That's what she noticed first.

It seemed a miracle, but H had somehow found a large, fallen log against an embankment that had created a sort of shelter. It wasn't waterproof, and it was a tight fit with both of them lying side by side. But H had insisted Sparrow be on the inside, as much out of the rain as possible. He'd crowded her against the damp earth, fallen tree behind her shoulder, and turned his back to the world outside.

They'd both lain awake for hours. Listening to the ebb and flow of the rain during the long night. She wasn't sure the rain had ever stopped.

It was still drizzling now. The quiet woods coming slowly into focus felt ethereal.

H slept on. One of his arms rested heavy over her waist and anchored her.

She was sure she had cobwebs in her hair and that she was covered in mud. What she wouldn't give for a hot bath.

She breathed deeply of peat and damp air as a memory rolled over her. Ma washing her in a round tub of warm, sudsy water. Laughing and splashing. She'd been small. Maybe five.

Memories had been slipping into place all throughout

the quiet hours of the night. H had shared his terrible memory with her and been quiet ever since.

She had to wonder if whatever had caused the memory loss—the berries, as H had suggested?—was wearing off. Her memories had cascaded and ebbed but when she reached for more current ones—her wedding to H, her name—they slipped away.

H made a small noise in his throat. She held her breath, wondering whether he'd wakened.

The gray light was just enough for her to see his features, slack in sleep. The proud curve of his nose, the stubble at his jaw. The lips that had kissed her so passionately. The shadow of his lashes against his cheeks.

His name hovered on her lips, just out of reach.

But another memory overtook her with breathless grief. Herself standing at the edge of a grave, newly mounded with dirt. She must've been all of fifteen. Joseph stood beside her, silent. Holding his cap in both hands.

How was she meant to go on without her mam in her life? Mam had been a steady presence, wise and gracious and always ready with a kind word. She'd taught Sparrow how to cook. How many hours had they worked in the kitchen together over the years since Sparrow had been a wee child?

The hot knife of grief sliced through her chest as if reliving that moment.

"Chin up." Those had been her brother's words.

Her chin wobbled when she turned her gaze on him, unable to move more than her head. If she walked away, if she left, then it became real. Mam wasn't coming back. Not ever.

Joseph's eyes had been awash in tears. "Mr. Smith told

me just this morning that he'll take you on as cook in Mam's place."

Sparrow's throat grew hot imagining being in that kitchen, where Mam had worked these past five years, without the woman she loved so dearly.

I can't.

But the words remained stuck behind her throat. Sparrow was afraid if she opened her mouth, only wails would emerge.

Joseph's hands flexed on his hat and then he reached out to touch her shoulder. "It's a good job, with good pay. The Smith family treats us fairly."

She knew that he meant the words to be a comfort, that she should count the job as a blessing. Without it, she would have nowhere to stay, no income.

But she didn't want the job. She wanted mam back.

Everything that had seemed true, that Mam would always be by her side, had been wrong. Sparrow didn't know how to go on, not when the ground had been torn from beneath her feet.

"Chin up."

It was a small mercy when the memory faded. She'd taken her brother's directive to heart. She'd worn a smile through those darkest days. It had taken years before any smile on her face had felt genuine. But she'd sung while she'd cooked, if only to feel Mam close.

She'd smiled and she'd poured herself into the job. And then Joseph had left her behind, as well. The memory she'd gained yesterday took on a new meaning, seeing Joseph off at the train platform.

She hadn't felt this layer of it yesterday, hadn't known

how the grief of her brother leaving had choked her. How she'd hidden it behind a smile.

Her leg twitched. She felt the slide of damp fabric against her skin. She wasn't soaking wet anymore. H's body against hers had provided warmth through the night. But the damp, uncomfortable feeling remained.

Her brow furrowed as she focused on his face again. If H had left with her brother on that train, where had they gone? When had he returned? And where was Joseph now?

With the strength of returning memories, she pushed—

And found a deluge. What felt like all of them.

Herself on the train. Leaving behind everything she'd known in the East. The rough and tumble town of Independence.

Meeting Felicity and taking charge of their wagon.

Felicity!

What had happened to her friend? Had she weathered last night's storm? She was married now. To August.

August.

Owen.

Leo.

Alice.

Each one of the travelers in their company had become a friend during the course of their journey. They'd worked together, mourned the loss of Evangeline's father. Survived a twister. A buffalo stampede.

A certainty sank deep inside her. Her friends wouldn't have stopped looking for her. They would never have left her behind.

A new anticipation shimmered. Surely with the territory she and H had covered yesterday, they must've drawn closer to the wagon train. Even if the company had moved on, unable to wait, August—the best tracker in the company—would be looking for them.

She could see the jovial, quiet man clearly in her mind's eye. Memories continued to settle and click into place.

"Abigail." The memory of August calling her name .

She gasped softly.

Abigail Fletcher. She had a name. Not Sparrow, though she had grown fond of the nickname Hollis had given her.

Hollis.

His name clicked into place as she stared at his dear face —and remembered everything.

Memories of him holding her, warming her by the fire two nights ago warred with a memory of him snapping at her to *leave him be* when she'd confronted him about the gaps in his memory from the head injury he'd sustained.

Worry slithered through her as more memories came to light. Had his head been injured again last night? She didn't know a lot about head wounds, but Maddie's caution from weeks ago was suddenly fresh on her mind.

Hollis frowning at her when she'd been singing as she'd washed clothing in camp.

Not looking at her when she'd delivered his meal to him when he'd been bedridden after his injury.

Hollis wasn't her husband.

They weren't married at all.

She wasn't even sure he would consider her a friend.

He'd told her when she'd joined the company in Independence that he was only allowing her there because Joseph had written and begged Hollis to watch over her. Joseph had sent funds for her journey after Mr. Smith had stolen all the savings she'd set aside for the long trip west.

Now the weight of Hollis's arm around her waist felt wrong. Embarrassment warred with shame. When Hollis's memories returned, he'd realize just how mistaken they'd been about their relationship.

He might even come to hate her—

She couldn't stop the sharp inhale as the gravity of everything he'd shared with her last night sank in. Hollis was a deeply private person. He'd shared one of his most painful memories with her. Not only the words but the pain and grief as she'd held him close.

When he remembered who she was to him—no one— and what he'd told her, he might be angry.

She couldn't be sure whether it was the breathless grief of losing her mam all over again or the loss of the tenuous relationship she'd formed with Hollis, but tears welled in her eyes.

Now she had a new reason to push for every mile they could make today. The sooner they reunited with the company, Abigail would be with her friends and Hollis with August and Owen, who seemed to be the only ones he let close.

When his memories returned, everything would change.

Seven

H'S STOMACH growled as he trudged along several yards beside the riverbank.

Sparrow walked beside and slightly behind him. Surely she was hungry, too. Yesterday around midday, they had eaten the fish he'd caught at their original camp. He hadn't stopped to fish again, not with the river water muddy and murky.

Not when someone might be trailing them.

The ground was already dry. Still hard, as if the torrential rainfall had run off instead of soaking in. The rain had been of little help to the parched grass all around. They'd passed through the charred remains of grass that had been scorched by the wildfire. He guessed it had been lit by one of the strikes of lightning. Last night, they'd seemed so close. Too close.

He didn't want to think about that now.

When he glanced at Sparrow, her mouth formed a moue of determination, her eyes on the horizon in front of them. She'd been quiet all morning, and it unsettled him.

He'd felt it from the first moment he'd come awake—he hadn't meant to fall asleep, the two of them wedged under that fallen tree that had become a makeshift shelter—as she'd pulled out of his arms. He'd been experiencing a vivid dream—a memory?—of lying in a bed, covered by the quilt, next to his wife, their fingers threaded together. He'd just been about to glance into her face—Sparrow's face?—when he'd been awakened by the movement of her drawing away.

She'd disappeared into some scrub brush for a few moments of privacy, and when she'd returned, he could tell something had changed. Whatever was bothering her, she wasn't sharing.

When hunger pangs had him gathering the fishing line and whittled hook from his pocket, she'd been the one to insist they start walking early, that there would be time to eat later.

It was probably for the best.

He caught the tail end of a glance from Sparrow, but when he turned his face toward her, she kept her eyes focused ahead as she picked her way around a stand of spiny shrubs.

The determination was new. H had been the one pushing yesterday. He could only guess how many miles they'd gone. His feet still ached from it.

Today, he felt resigned. If they hadn't found any sign of a camp or wagon train yesterday, just how far had they been washed downstream?

Worse, he'd realized not long after they'd started walking this morning that any tracks or sign of others likely would've been washed away by the strong rains. If anyone was out looking for them, the scouts might miss them altogether.

The only thing that kept him pushing this morning was the knowledge that whoever had attacked him last night was still out there. He couldn't keep from glancing over his shoulder. He felt as if there was a target painted on his back. And underneath it all was a blanket of grief over the memory that had surfaced last night. Charles's last breaths. His laugh. Missing him in every moment.

The quiet became too much. H blurted, "If we don't find a place to fish soon, it might be best to stop and figure how to lay a snare. It might take some time, but we could catch a rabbit or some other critter."

Her eyes darted to him and then back to the horizon. She worried her bottom lip between her teeth.

He hadn't heard her humming all morning. He hadn't realized it was bothering him until the moment it became clear in his mind. He'd grown used to her sweet notes as she'd hiked along all day yesterday and a few times the day before in their camp. Now it was like an itch he couldn't scratch.

She pointed toward the western horizon. Still didn't stop. "Don't you think we should keep moving? Surely we must be catching up with the company by now."

There seemed to be both an urgency and a worry in her statement.

"I'm a little concerned," he confessed. "They may have moved on without us. We know we've been on our own for at least three days. And last night's rain would've washed away any tracks—ours or those of a company. Maybe they think we're dead. Maybe they've left."

Yet the statement felt off, like a chime ringing in his head at the wrong frequency.

She shook her head, her lips firming. "I—I regained more of my memories early this morning."

She had? The momentary elation was eclipsed by the question of why she hadn't mentioned it before now. They'd been up and moving for at least two hours.

Her eyes darted away from his glance. Had she remembered something unsavory about their relationship? Had they been in a fight when they'd been swept away by the river? His next step crunched a burned clump of grass.

"I remembered our company," she said tightly. "Our friends. Owen Mason, one of your captains. And August, his brother. A talented scout."

She glanced at him questioningly, but he shook his head. The names didn't unlock anything in his shadowy memories. They were simply names.

"Felicity, the woman—" She cut herself off. "My friend." At her side, her hand flexed and then balled into a fist. "They wouldn't leave us behind."

She sounded certain. Enough that he wanted to believe her, even if he had no memories of his own of these people she spoke of.

"You remembered a lot," he murmured.

She rubbed a hand over her brow, leaving a streak of mud high on her left cheek. "I think... I think before the crossing, we were traveling on that side of the river." She waved across the span of the churning water. "I remember falling in. My wagon brushed against a beehive. Bees started stinging me—and the oxen. You were on your horse..."

He closed his hand over hers and she blinked out of the

memory. Her breaths had grown more rapid. He didn't want her to be frightened, not now.

"What are our names?" His voice contained a breathless note. A sense of being on a precipice. Her words stirred something inside him.

He used her hand to tug her to a stop, to force her to face him.

Her eyes were big in her face. "My name is Abigail."

She watched him closely. He wished that hearing her name unlocked his memories. He wanted to have them. The wedding that he'd remembered snatches of. How they'd met. All the moments in between.

Disappointment flickered in her eyes, echoing his own feelings. She smiled flatly.

"And you are Hollis Tremblay. The wagon master of our company."

She said more, but the words didn't register as he was thrown into a memory.

"Hollis, grab the tongs."

"I remember my pa," he breathed. He hadn't meant to tighten his grip on her hand, but he was clinging to her as the memory washed over him and reality faded.

All of fifteen, working in the livery with Pa. The two of them repairing a carriage, working with the axle and wheels.

The clouds of grief over losing Charles had only started to pass.

There was something else there.

A man rushed into the livery, spewing mad.

"You rented me a bad horse."

Hollis knew the horse. It was Hollis's own beloved chestnut gelding, the one he'd raised from a colt. A fine animal, if sensitive.

The details of the conversation between the man and Hollis's pa blurred as Hollis realized what had happened—his horse had been injured.

He ran through the city streets to where the lane changed to open country—and saw his horse lying prone..

A profound silence blocked out everything else in a rush of white.

His horse, his friend, was gone.

Hollis came back into the present with tears on his face. Abigail reached up to brush them away.

How much of that had he said aloud? Enough, because she was blinking back tears of her own.

"What a terrible tragedy," she breathed.

But when he reached for her, wanting to draw her near, needing the comfort of someone he loved in his arms, she stayed him with a hand at his chest.

"Wait."

His emotions tumbled. Why was she pulling away? He couldn't understand—

"There's something you should know."

He didn't want to know. Whatever was broken between them, there in the shadows of his memories, he'd fix it. He looked over her head, his eyes unfocused as emotion surged. And saw a man in the far distance, on horseback.

Abigail felt the sudden tension in Hollis where they were still connected by their hands.

For a moment, she thought that perhaps his own

memories had returned, but then she noticed he was staring over her head.

She was turning to see what he was looking at when his arm banded around her waist.

"Let's hide in the trees," he said urgently. "It might be the man from last night."

An echo of the stark terror she'd felt when she'd realized that Hollis was grappling with the other man trembled through her. She allowed herself to be pulled in the direction of the nearest patch of woods but couldn't resist craning her neck for one look over her shoulder.

She stopped dead. "Hollis!" She clutched his shoulder. "That's August. That's his horse."

She'd recognize the buckskin mare anywhere, even if the man himself was only a dark smudge at this distance.

"You absolutely sure?" Hollis demanded. He held onto her waist, his strength keeping her from breaking out into a sprint.

August meant safety. They must be close to the company! Though it came to her in an instant that August usually ranged far and wide when he was tracking.

Hollis had told her that the rains last night would erase any kind of tracks. If they had any hope of reuniting with the company, they needed to catch August's attention.

"Here!" she shouted. Hollis's arm fell away from her waist. She waved her arms, aware of him behind her. "We're here!"

The scream left her throat feeling hoarse, and she was quickly out of breath as she jumped and waved both arms.

"He can't hear you." Hollis moved behind her. What was he doing, why wasn't he—?

She couldn't tear her eyes away from August's horse.

She realized he was getting smaller, moving away from them.

"No!" desperation leaked out in her voice.

"I'm going to fire a signal shot," Hollis warned.

She finally turned and saw he'd taken his gun out of its holster. He was pointing it toward the ground, away from both of them.

Even though he'd warned her, the crack of the shot echoed in her chest as she stared at the far off rider.

The horse wheeled.

The moment seemed to stretch long as she waited, breathless.

And then a quiet sound, one that seemed to barely reach their ears.

The crack of another shot.

They'd been heard.

Slowly, August grew bigger. She couldn't contain herself. She ran toward him. She could feel Hollis following, then became aware of his strained breath, probably from his injuries last night. All morning long, she hadn't missed how gingerly he moved, how his ribs pained him.

She slowed to a fast walk, sending a concerned glance his way.

More horsemen joined August, and her heart leapt. She'd been right when she'd told Hollis that their company wouldn't abandon them in the wilderness.

As the men neared, she recognized Owen. And a cowboy–Gerry Bones, recognizable because of the stained white ten-gallon hat he wore to shade his brown-skinned face. And Mr. Beaumont, another traveler with the company that she didn't know as well. Beaumont's pale blue shirt was a contrast to his brown skin with golden undertones.

August slid off his horse before the animal had plodded to a stop.

"Hollis! Abigail!"

She ran and threw her arms around him. She couldn't say whether she'd ever hugged him before, but the moment his arms closed around her in a brief hug, sweet relief flowed through her. Tears sprang to her eyes. She laughed a little as one slipped free. She took a step back.

"Are we glad to see you," August said.

Owen was off his horse, his hand clasping Hollis's wrist in a firm clasp. The two other men were still dismounting.

"We found Abigail's wagon, deduced that you two had been swept away in the river," Owen said.

August had turned back to his horse. Now he pulled out something wrapped in a handkerchief. He unfolded it to reveal a biscuit, golden and floury.

He gave it to Abigail, who broke it in two and handed one half to Hollis. His eyes said his thanks as he stuffed it in his mouth.

Mr. Beaumont approached, shrewd black eyes taking them in.

"Some of the company thought you were dead," Beaumont said. "Jes' like before."

Abigail shuddered. August saw, shifted closer.

"You all right?" he asked low.

"We didn't know what had happened for a couple days," she told him. She explained about their memories, about the vomit they'd seen, their conclusion about the berries.

Sometime in the middle of her explanation, August had pulled a blanket from behind his saddle and wrapped it around her. It smelled clean and faintly of horse, and she realized just how badly she needed a bath and her dress and underthings laundered. The warmth from the blanket seeped in to her skin, still damp from their night in the rain.

"His memories haven't come back?" August asked her, voice low.

The other three men had clustered around Hollis and Abigail was content to be half-hidden behind August's horse, blocked from their rapid-fire conversation peppered with words like, "wildfire" and "flooding."

Now that she and Hollis had been found, she was terribly conscious of how it looked for two unmarried travelers to be alone in the wild together for several days.

Beaumont glanced at her over his shoulder, curiosity evident in his expression.

"...came across a man on horseback, a small camp," Hollis was saying.

August cupped her shoulder momentarily and then edged toward the other men.

"Did you get a look at him?" Owen pressed. "I've heard rumor someone might be tracking our company, but neither August or I have seen any sign to indicate he was close."

She saw the flicker of uncertainty cross Hollis's expression. He must've noticed how the men were looking to him for leadership. "It was dark. I only had a glimpse of his face once, when lightning flashed."

She edged toward August. "August—"

He glanced at her. "We need to get these two back to

camp. I'm sure they're half starved and in want of a real bed."

Owen nodded decisively. "We can double up. The horses won't be able to travel fast, but the two of you must be worn plumb out after everything you've endured."

Hollis's expression softened. "Sparrow—Abigail kept our spirits up with her singing and humming."

Owen shot a confused glance between the two of them. "You... liked it?"

"Why wouldn't I like my wife's voice?"

The moment the words left Hollis's mouth, Abigail stifled a gasp.

August showed no surprise, but shock was clearly written on Owen's face, along with the other two men.

Hollis had claimed her as his wife. The deductions the two of them had made were the influence of their proximity and those berries. And they'd been wrong. His claim wasn't true.

What was she supposed to do now?

Eight

ALICE HAULED another quilt to the stream. The material was damp and dirty, a casualty of the flooding rains they'd endured in the night.

She'd lost count of how many muddy bedrolls, articles of clothing, and dishes she'd washed this morning. She was tired from a sleepless night, still felt residual echoes from the fear of near tragedy.

She wasn't the only one feeling unsettled. The women and older children from the company marching like a line of ants, to and from the small pool on the edge of the river that held mostly-clear water, wore shadowed faces. The river had almost taken a little boy. Would've swept him away if it hadn't been for Alice's sister-in-law Rachel and her quick thinking.

She'd overheard her brothers Leo and Owen talking this morning before the sun had come up. If the search parties didn't find Hollis and Abigail today, they had to assume the travelers were dead. That's what Leo had said.

His voice had broken when he'd said it.

Alice's own heart felt like it was breaking. Abigail was her friend. She'd been missing for four days. Was it possible she was still alive somewhere out in the wild?

If anyone could survive out there, it was Hollis. He'd take care of her.

The pool was quiet, its bank empty of other travelers when Alice arrived, and that was a small mercy. She swiped her forehead with the back of one wrist. A hot wind evaporated what rainwater hadn't run off. The ground was nearly dry again—little good the storm had done.

Alice swung the blanket out, letting it unfurl before it floated to land on top of the water before it began to sink under the surface. The motion had pulled a small smile from her, but in the very next moment, the blanket snagged on something below. It jerked in Alice's hands and she fought to keep her footing on the grasses at the bank, still damp in this shady spot.

Her eyes slipped closed as she struggled with the blanket, pulling with all her might.

Was this how Rachel had felt last night, fighting against the raging river to save the young boy she'd rescued?

The memory locked in Alice's head, watching in horror as Rachel and the young boy clung to a tree as the waters threatened to sweep them under. Owen had rescued them both from horseback, just in the nick of time.

She blinked, pushing the memory away. Selfishly grateful that it hadn't been her.

Alice was a horrible person.

An awful person for being insincere when she'd formed a truce with her brother Owen's wife weeks ago. It irked her that her brothers were caught up in their new relationships. Who was going to watch out for Coop while they were domestically distracted?

It was all up to her.

And she wished that it wasn't.

Which made her selfish.

She opened her eyes and gave one more tug on the heavy quilt. A little cry slipped from her lips. The blanket didn't budge and helplessness itched just under her skin. She couldn't afford to lose the covering.

Then a pair of big hands grabbed the blanket just below where she held it. She only caught a glimpse of the side of Braddock's face as he pulled with her.

Finally, something shifted under the eddying water and the blanket came loose. His hands brushed hers as she pulled it in.

"I've got it," she told him, shaken by his sudden appearance.

He stepped back, pushing one hand through his hair—where was his hat?—as he watched her tug the waterlogged blanket to shore.

She didn't want to notice the bruise high on his cheek or the one shading his jaw underneath a scruff of blond whiskers. He was staring at her, watching her take in the evidence of the blows her brother had landed two days ago.

Are you all right? The old Alice, the girl she'd been eight months ago, would've asked the question. But she firmed her lips and purposely returned her focus to the blanket, now on dry ground. She knelt to examine a small rip that now marred the edge.

"I'm fine," he said after a prolonged moment of silence. "Thank you for asking." One corner of his mouth lifted, a sign that he hadn't meant anything unkind by the sarcastic words.

Of course he pushed. Braddock—she couldn't think of him as Robert anymore—always pushed.

"What do you want?" she asked as she wound the quilt between her hands, wringing water from it.

"To talk to you."

"I told you, I never want to see you again." If she blinked, she'd be back in the servant's hallway of his grandfather's expansive mansion, facing him with tear-filled eyes. She shook her head, freeing herself from the memory.

"You also told me you loved me," he said in a matter-of-fact tone, his jaw hard and his arms crossed over his chest. "Both of those things can't be true. One of them must be a lie."

His words battered her for a moment, tugging at her insides the way the quilt had been pulled by the water. She had thought herself in love with him once. But she'd only been fooling herself.

"I love my brother, but I don't love his foolish actions," she said evenly. It was as close to an apology as she could make. She knew the truth now—how he truly felt about her family. About her station.

Water spattered over her skirt as she squeezed the fabric too strongly, her emotions getting the better of her. She could never be with Braddock. It would never work between them. The evidence of it was there in the bruises on his face.

And it wasn't only that Leo, Collin, and Coop hated him.

When she looked up, she got caught in his blue eyes.

His expression was stony. He opened his mouth, then closed it again. A muscle jumped in his cheek.

"Whatever affection we used to have for each other is gone," she said firmly. "I don't know what foolish notion brought you to this wagon train, but you should join the next eastbound group and go home to your grandfather."

"It's not gone for me." He strode forward and before she could react took the bottom of the sopping mass of blanket before she dropped it all on the dirty ground. His hands found hers in the process, and she found she couldn't look away from his intent gaze.

"It's not gone for me," he repeated.

The warmth of his hands closing over hers brought back a visceral memory of the first time he'd touched her—during a rousing song at one of the dances attended mostly by workers from the powder mill. They'd been pressed in on all sides by the crowd, and he'd held her hand for a moment too long during the spinning, clapping dance around them. He hadn't looked away, not even when he'd missed a step and nearly stumbled. She'd thought she was something special, to have captured the attention of a man like him.

You're different from your working class brothers!

His shouted words from another conversation—their last real conversation before this one—resounded through her buzzing ears. She stepped away, breaking his hold and tugging the blanket into her midsection, uncaring that she got her dress wet.

"You're the one who said we're too different," she reminded him stiffly. "And that hasn't changed. Leave me alone."

She walked briskly toward camp, blinded by tears. It

wasn't enough that her brothers had found love? Why did she have to come face to face with the proof that she'd made a huge mistake?

She'd believed love was bigger than the elements of their lives that separated them. She came from poverty, while he had been born with a silver spoon in his mouth. Their relationship had been secret for months. And hadn't survived when her brothers had been dismissed from Braddock's powder mill.

The dreams she'd had of being Braddock's wife, of home and love and babies had died. All of them.

She didn't look over her shoulder to the man she left behind.

There was no reason to look back. Nothing left for them to say.

* * *

Riding double, it wasn't long before the wagons came into sight. The white covers stood out against the sea of dry prairie grasses, and Abigail's eyes filled with grateful tears.

She had her hands on Hollis's waist. August had given up his horse for them to use while he rode double with Gerry Bones. Owen rode out front. She'd seen the troubled look he wore when Hollis had blurted out that she was his wife.

With her memories back, Abigail remembered the wagon master who'd driven himself to the brink of exhaustion pushing the wagon train west. Who'd hidden the continued pain and weakness from the head injury he'd received when the twister had come through weeks ago.

Hollis hated to show weakness.

When his memories returned, he would be angry with himself for what he'd revealed to the four men who'd made up the search party.

Hollis's posture atop the horse filled with more and more tension as they approached the caravan.

"You all right?" she asked.

She thought she heard him whisper, "Ten lost," but couldn't be sure.

Owen reined in near a group of several horses picketed outside the circle of wagons. Only a few seconds later, he held the bridle as Hollis hooked one arm around Abigail to let her down. She couldn't help one last look at the man who'd kept her safe these past days. Hollis sat tall and strong in the saddle. Capable and handsome.

He'd held her, protected her with his own body. Shared himself with her.

And now all of that was over.

She clutched August's blanket closer around her shoulders. Nearby, the camp bustled with activity and movement. For a moment, she felt separated, out of place.

August appeared at her side. "We've got two other search parties ranging the prairie. They're supposed to check in at the noon hour."

She nodded. No doubt the caravan would need to move on soon.

"Owen wants to grab Leo for a captains' meeting. To figure out what to do next."

When she glanced at August, his eyes were on Owen and Hollis, feet away and, from the looks of it, having a serious conversation.

She and August had only met after the company left Independence. They had been acquaintances for weeks, until they'd bonded over worry for their wagon master, who'd been found with a head injury after the twister.

"He'll need a friend by his side, once his memories return." She murmured the words as she hugged the blanket tighter around her. "It could happen at any moment."

August's mouth pulled in a frown. "It's a shame it couldn't have happened before we found you."

She knew he meant before Hollis had told everyone what he had.

August's gaze held compassion. "Folks'll want to see the two of you. Everyone's been worried. I'd keep to yourself for as long as you can."

So Hollis can't spread more untruths. She heard the words he didn't say. It was sound advice.

Hollis and Owen walked ahead, while August stayed to speak to the cowpoke and care for their horses. Abigail trailed the two men.

As they passed through the wagons, Owen spoke to a woman—Felicity.

She abandoned the bucket and scrub brush and jumped to her feet to meet Abigail.

"You're alive!"

Abigail gave in to her friend's embrace, new tears stinging her eyes as Felicity's arms wrapped around her.

"I'm a muddy mess," Abigail tried to warn her.

But Felicity kept one arm around her. "We all are. Those storms last night nearly flooded our camp—we almost lost a little boy who'd wondered off."

Terror filled Abigail as she relived those moments of being pulled underwater by the current. A flash of Hollis's strong arm clasping her waist, dragging her to the surface—

She pushed the memory away. Focused instead on the woman nearby who had removed every item from her wagon and was standing inside it, beneath the empty slats, no cover, sweeping water out. Their canvas must've leaked.

Another family worked to dig out their wagon wheels from the soft, muddy ground.

"Is my wagon all right?" Abigail asked.

Felicity nodded. "Your oxen must've dragged it across the river. After you disappeared, some of the men found it on the banks, the oxen just waiting in their traces."

Abigail's stomach chose that moment to growl and Felicity's eyes went wide. "Oh my goodness. You must be so hungry. Let me—"

But Alice was already striding toward them, a tin plate in her hand. "I just saw Owen. He sent me over here."

She hugged Abigail's shoulders with one arm before handing her the plate. "I was so worried about you. What happened?"

It was a relief to give herself into the care of her friends. To sit on a crate they pushed her to, and let them warm up pails of water for her to get cleaned up.

She was embarrassed at how she ate. Head down, stuffing her mouth like some kind of animal, all to appease her roaring stomach.

Had someone made sure Hollis was eating?

She held the question inside, August's warning echoing in her mind.

Felicity and Alice listened wide-eyed as she told the story of the past few days in between bites. But she kept the tender moments with Hollis to herself.

"Abigail!" The cry, somewhere between a shriek and a

wail, preceded a bundle of energy in the form of Ben flying in.

Abigail's blanket fell away as she braced and then caught the nine-year-old girl in her arms. Ben had come to the wagon train a few weeks ago, after her own company had been attacked by bandits and her family killed. Felicity and August had taken her in, but the girl had formed a special bond with Abigail.

Abigail hadn't realized how deeply she'd missed the girl and blinked back tears.

Ben drew back with a wrinkled nose. "You stink."

"Ben!" Felicity gasped. "Manners."

Abigail stifled a teary laugh. "I'm certain I do. I'm in terrible need of a bath."

Alice hefted one of the pails from the now-roaring fire. "We've got a washtub fixed up. Strung blankets between our two wagons for privacy."

There was a relief in allowing herself to lean on her friends. These past days, it had been Abigail and Hollis alone. No supplies, no food, no idea where they should go.

"How did you survive with only a grumpy Gus for company?" Felicity teased.

"We managed together," Abigail murmured.

The stark fear she'd carried since she'd woken up without her memory had started to bleed away the moment August had ridden up to them out on the prairie. Even so, she was conscious of the words trapped behind her sternum. She wanted to tell Felicity everything. But the secrets of what she'd been through, what she and Hollis had shared, were hers alone.

Hunger sated, she allowed herself to be led to her bath. Alice continued talking, but the words faded behind the blankets as Abigail hesitated. Hollis sat near a low-burning fire, surrounded by his captains. And... Evangeline?

Evangeline had several guidebooks packed in her supplies, Abigail remembered. August had commented about how frivolous it had seemed that she, the daughter of a wealthy lumber magnate, had brought an entire library along in her wagon. But surely the guidebooks would be helpful now, with Hollis's memory impaired.

Hollis's shoulders were set and tense. She could see it from here, though his back was to her. Everyone would be depending on him, now that he'd returned. The responsibility was a big one when in his right state. But without his memories, was he feeling uncertain? Angry?

"Abby?" The nickname slipped from Alice's lips as she drew back the blanket. Behind her, a washtub was steaming. She'd laid a clean towel over the edge and now she offered Abigail a bar of sweet-smelling soap. "You okay?"

Abigail forced a smile, though it felt like it wasn't quite the right shape on her lips. "Fine. Just woolgathering."

Alice's gaze went past her. Abigail feared she'd see the men and guess at her seesawing emotions. She quickly ducked past her friend. "Thank you for the bath."

Alice murmured a response and left her there.

Abigail didn't want the hot water her friends had labored over to go to waste, so she quickly slipped into the tub. The warm water was a balm to her skin. The scent of the soap familiar and welcome. But thoughts of Hollis plagued her.

His strong arm coming around her when he'd dove into the raging river to rescue her.

The warmth of sharing his coat next to the fire.

The way he'd held her and comforted her.

His kiss, the way it'd claimed her.

What had been a friendship—and barely that—before they'd been separated from the company had become something more.

For her, at least.

She had no doubt that when Hollis's memory returned, any moment now, he'd hate the closeness they'd shared. He'd worked hard to keep everyone around him at arms' length. She doubted he'd told anyone else about the tragedies from his childhood. She knew more about him than anyone else. And he wouldn't like that. It wouldn't matter that she would never tell a soul.

Frustration rolled over her like a wave in the river, and she let herself slide down until her knees were sticking up out of the tub but her head was underwater.

With her eyes tightly closed and everything around her muted, she could pretend, if only for one moment, that things could be the same as they had before her memory had returned.

She'd liked belonging to Hollis.

* * *

It was growing dark by the time Hollis had a minute to wash up.

"You haven't had a moment to yourself."

August.

Hollis had repeated the man's name over and over in his mind so he would remember it.

The man—his friend?—approached where Hollis stood between two wagons looking out at the last sliver of the setting sun.

"What can I do for you?" Hollis asked.

August shook his head. He'd stuck close all day, covering for Hollis when the blanks in his memory might've troubled the other travelers. It hadn't been until midday that Hollis realized he hadn't told Owen or Beaumont or Gerry Bones that his memories were gone.

August had something in his hands and held it out now, offering it to Hollis.

Clothes, he realized. A rough towel, a bar of soap. August extended his other hand. A straight razor. A flicker of some recognition fluttered inside Hollis as he took it.

"Most of the men bathe down by the river, though the water isn't very clean after the storms." A gentle suggestion in the words.

Hollis thanked him with a nod.

August hesitated. "You doing all right? With everything?"

"Fine."

"I'm sure things'll be easier after a good night's rest," August offered.

Hollis looked down at the things in his hands. He felt bone tired—more so than when he'd walked all day and slept on the bare ground. Everyone wanted something from him.

Two families had asked him to mediate a dispute about whether or not the faulty piece of canvas one family had loaned the other could be blamed for the leak in their wagon.

His captains had wanted to discuss the upcoming route for what seemed like hours. One of the men—Hollis couldn't remember his name now—had asked Hollis outright why he hadn't pulled out his logbook. Their arguing and debating had stirred up something in Hollis, something just out of reach.

The one silver lining was that one of the other search parties had found his horse. He'd gone out to greet the animal and recognized the gelding straightaway. His mount had been half-wild, spirits high and still wearing his saddle, with many of Hollis's supplies intact and his rifle still in the scabbard. Hollis had seen to his care, those few minutes spent in familiar tasks his only respite, until now.

"Where's Spar—Abigail?" He wasn't sure he would get used to calling her by her Christian name, not when Sparrow had become so familiar in his mind. "In our tent?"

A look crossed August's features, one that Hollis couldn't read. "She's bedded down with Felicity—my wife —and young Ben. Probably already asleep."

A visceral need inside him made him say, "I need to see her. Make sure she's all right."

August stayed him with a hand at his chest when Hollis would've pushed past the man. "I'm... not sure she wants that."

Hollis shook his head, not comprehending the other man's words.

"Hollis, sir." August was two inches shorter, but Hollis had to give it to him, he didn't back down.

"I've a right to check on my wife."

August was married. Surely he understood that.

Some shadow crossed the man's expression in the last of the light.

"What?" Hollis demanded.

"She's not your wife."

The words didn't register. Not until August followed them with, "You and Abigail aren't married."

Of course we are. The argument pressed against his breastbone, but didn't reach his mouth.

Was this why Abigail hadn't come to him today?

He didn't believe it.

"Why don't you go wash up?" August suggested firmly. "Making a ruckus this time of night isn't a good idea. I'll come find you by the creek and let you know how she is."

Hollis wanted to argue, but he became aware of others passing nearby, men on watch. Listening ears.

He trudged out into the darkness, finding his way to the water's edge by sound. It took a minute to find a place where the water was calm enough that he could scoop some into his hands.

He shucked his mud-encrusted shirt. Set aside the razor. It was too dark tonight to shave. He'd save that for the morning.

Abigail isn't your wife.

His heart was pounding against his sternum, almost like fighting the man who'd attacked him out there in the wild.

He'd been sure. Felt the certainty. But she'd been quiet since her memories had returned. Had she known? And kept it from him? What about the memories of his bride—?

He had his hands cupped around a bit of water when the first of the memories swarmed him, overtaking his vision with scenes from the past. He lost his grip on the water and his hands splashed into the edge of the water, then gripped the ground at his knees, gaining purchase on one solid thing as his mind swam.

His pa and ma, looking proud from the back of the

crowd as he'd recited words in a spelling bee. He must've been around ten.

Running through the night, belly empty, when he was even smaller. They'd left behind a life of slavery in the south. A wash of memories of Hollis's pa, the shadows in his eyes that time and distance had never truly erased.

Hollis's own wedding day.

But it wasn't Abigail who turned to face him in that pretty dress. It was Dinah, her warm brown skin and dark brown eyes serious as she took his hand in front of the preacher.

His heart twisted strongly inside him and he gasped for breath, the memories pressing against the inside of his skull.

Dinah making dinner in their tiny kitchen. Bringing him a lunch pail at the livery. Growing big with their child.

Dinah's screams.

Hollis's helplessness as the doctor tried to save her and the baby.

Tried and failed.

Grief overwhelmed him, the memories new again, as if they were happening right now, not five years ago. He'd loved Dinah with all his heart, loved their unborn baby.

And God had taken both of them in one fell swoop.

Hollis groaned. It came from the depths of his soul, but it didn't lessen the pain, only heightened it.

A twig snapped beneath someone's boot and he pushed himself to stand on shaky legs. Forced himself to turn, though his stomach pitched.

August picked his way through the brush with a lantern in his hand. And he wasn't alone. Abigail was just behind him.

Hollis rubbed one hand down his face. "Go away." His voice was rough with tears and pain, and it shamed him that they heard.

Abigail stopped short, but August took two more steps.

Abigail's face was a pale smudge in the flickering lantern light, but Hollis could see her eyes, wide and hurt and full of compassion.

"You knew," he accused her, the words bubbling out of his mouth before they'd fully formed in his mind.

"Only since this morning," she whispered.

"How could you let me pretend?" *Let me kiss you?* He knew it wasn't her fault, somewhere in the back of his brain, but in this moment logic had no place.

He saw the tremble before she hid her hands in the folds of her skirt.

A visceral memory hit him, a recent one. Holding onto her in the dark. Because she felt precious to him. Some part of him ached to hold her now. He hated himself for it.

"Hollis," August started.

He pointed a shaking finger at her. "You aren't my wife." His voice shook. "My wife and our baby are dead."

She looked stricken. Her lip trembled. "Oh, Hollis."

He didn't know where his self control had gone. Surely he hadn't meant to tell her about Dinah. His family back home knew, but no one in the caravan.

"Hollis, let us help you through this."

He batted away August's hand when the man came near enough to touch him.

He couldn't stop staring at Abigail. She'd seen him weak. Vulnerable. Heard his darkest secrets.

"We did what we had to in order to survive," he told

her. "But you tell no one what happened out there. No one."

She turned her face, giving him her profile. In the dim lantern light, he saw the glint of tears in her eyes.

"Let's go back to the company," August said. "Get some rest. We'll regroup in the morning."

Hollis's head pounded as he reached down to gather his things from the bank. He hadn't bathed, but maybe that didn't matter anymore.

His hands wouldn't stop shaking.

Tell no one.

His traitorous brain was quick to remind him of the statement he'd made when they'd been rescued. He'd claimed Abigail was his wife in front of August, Owen, Beaumont and Bones.

He'd created a problem. One that had no solution.

Nine

THE USUAL MORNING noise from camp was familiar, but something about the familiar was grating today. Part of Abigail missed the gurgling of the river, the quiet birdcalls.

Hollis's closeness.

She worked to put that from her mind as she took the pan of biscuits away from the campfire.

"Oh." Alice had come around the corner of one of the wagons and nearly ran into Abigail. "I didn't know you were there."

Abigail nodded acknowledgement. No harm done.

Alice waved a book in the air as she stepped around the fire. "Leaving this for Hollis. Leo wanted him to have it."

Good. Hollis's captains were rallying around him. Whether he would let anyone close was a mystery, but he needed friends.

Alice left the book on the open tailgate of Hollis's wagon. She was hurrying out of camp, obviously in the middle of packing up, but hesitated. "You're awfully quiet this morning. Everything all right?"

Abigail felt a shadow of herself. Or maybe it was the grief from regained memories that hung over her like a cloud. It wasn't good if Alice had noticed.

She attempted a smile. "Just feeling a little discombobulated being back in camp. I'll be all right."

Alice watched her with serious eyes. "You certain?"

Abigail nodded. "Every day on the trail is one day closer to seeing my brother."

That was the reason, Abigail realized, she had come on this journey. She needed to focus on Joseph, on her future. But she couldn't find the hope she'd felt before she'd left her home in the East. The unsettled, bitter memory of Mr. Smith's betrayal was too fresh. New again with the return of her memory.

Alice didn't seem to notice Abigail's uneasy attitude. She ducked out of the campsite, no doubt off on another errand. Abigail moved to the tailgate of her wagon where she'd set out several tin plates. She pushed for a sound from her throat. It was difficult to think of the tune, to begin to hum.

She felt much the same as she had after her mam had passed away.

Her skin prickled with constant awareness. No matter what she did, an ache knotted her stomach.

Chin up.

Joseph's voice in her head reminded her that there was no room for sadness. Not with so much to be done.

She didn't understand it. How could she be grieving the loss of a... friendship... with Hollis when it hadn't been real?

But it had felt real. When they'd fought against the elements, fought for survival, it'd been the two of them against the entire wilderness.

She blinked away the memories and realized she'd stopped humming again.

She let a tune vibrate from her throat, louder this time, as she spooned gravy over the biscuits. They'd been on the trail long enough that there were no bits of ham in the white gravy. This morning, she'd been conscious of the fact that the salt barrel was half-empty too. She'd been a little more stingy with the salt and pepper in the gravy. Were they halfway through this ordeal?

With nothing left but to serve the breakfast, she harrumphed when she realized her humming had faded again.

She strode through the camp, aware of a woman in conversation with her neighbor, a whisper cut off as Abigail walked past them. A man and his teenaged daughter stared at her as she progressed through camp.

She tried to shake off the uncomfortable feeling of being watched. It was only simple curiosity, she told herself. She simply wasn't used to being back in camp yet.

Hollis stood in conversation with Leo and another one of his captains. His head turned toward her. He must've seen her approach. But the moment their eyes met, he turned his face away.

Her breath felt caught in her chest at his slight—but it was the deeper punch of hurt from remembering his face in the lantern light last night, down by the river, that made the place behind her nose burn. The hurt felt as physical as a cut, but she pushed a trembling smile to her lips. She placed the tin plate atop a barrel behind Hollis with just a bit too much force before she whirled and strode away.

She hadn't known Hollis had been married. That he'd lost his wife and his unborn baby. What kind of woman had captured the taciturn man's attention? Hollis was a dynamic leader. Had his wife been just as commanding?

Abigail brushed her cheek, dodging a small child chasing a loose chicken. No tears had escaped, though her chest felt tight with pent up emotion.

Hollis hadn't shared any of his past with her willingly. She knew too much about him, had seen the depths of emotion he always kept hidden. That's why he'd turned his face away from her.

It still hurt.

Whatever hope she'd held onto that some thread of the friendship they'd forged out in the wild remained were now shredded.

As she packed away the cooking implements, she was aware of the movements of others in camp, the searching looks as folks gathered their belongings. The sun warmed things quickly. The dry wind brought to mind the smoke from the wildfire that had burned her throat and lungs.

The bugle blew. Only a few minutes left.

She hefted a heavy crate and had just placed it in the back of the wagon when someone called out to her. She turned, eyes assessing the campsite. Everything was tucked away, save Hollis's plate. He'd probably have someone else return it to her.

Rachel, Owen's wife, approached. Her tiny baby rested against her chest, wrapped in a thin blanket that crisscrossed Rachel's shoulders and somehow held the infant in place.

"Morning," Abigail greeted.

Rachel nodded. "Is there anything you need before we embark on today's leg?"

Abigail shook her head. "I heard you rescued a child—put yourself in peril to save him."

Rachel looked faintly embarrassed. "I'm glad to be back on dry land, that's for sure."

"It felt a little like we were in Noah's day, didn't it?" Abigail expected a smile at the joshing statement, but Rachel shifted her feet as if anxious about something. One hand rubbed up and down the sleeping baby's back.

"Owen asked me to speak to you," Rachel said finally. She exhaled a blustery breath and shook her head, color high on her cheeks. "I'm not used to being a captain's wife —not yet."

This was official business?

Abigail clasped her hands behind her back.

"There's been—some of the women, and men, gossiping about Hollis's statement that the two of you were married."

Abigail worked to keep her expression neutral. *That* was the reason for the covert glances she'd received all morning? For the whispers and abruptly ended conversations when she'd walked past? Frustration boiled inside her, but worry twisted her stomach.

"Owen is going to bring the matter to Hollis," Rachel said.

Abigail could only imagine what that conversation would entail. Hollis would be deeply unhappy to be the subject of gossip in his own wagon train.

"We'd like to ask—Owen and I—if you'd speak to Hollis as well. Let him know that he has our support, but that something needs to be done about this."

Abigail turned to lift and secure the tailgate, hoping the other woman wouldn't see her hand shaking on the rope tie. "I don't know that he wants to hear from me."

Not today. Maybe not ever.

Rachel cleared her throat. "I don't know what happened between you for those days you were missing..."

Abigail didn't respond to the leading statement. A quick quelling glance over her shoulder tightened Rachel's lips.

Abigail moved to the other end of the tailgate to secure it as well.

"Owen tells me that the last time Hollis was separated from the caravan, there was unrest."

The knot in Abigail's stomach pulled. It was true. When Hollis had been injured in the twister, the men had nearly come to blows about what course of action they should take next. But Hollis was back with the caravan now. Surely the men, everyone in the company, knew that their best chance of surviving this journey was under Hollis's leadership.

But Rachel didn't have to say any more for Abigail's thought to roll to each time people she'd thought sensible and intelligent had succumbed to their fear and made bad choices.

The wilderness wasn't merciful.

And she knew how Hollis took responsibility for every life under his care. She'd seen it firsthand when he'd taken such meticulous care of her. And many other times on the wagon train.

"Some families are talking about leaving the caravan," Rachel said urgently. "Waiting at the next fort until another caravan passes through." She sighed. "Please, can you try to talk to him?"

"Of course." Abigail's sharp answer seemed to placate Rachel, and as the first of the wagons began rolling out, Rachel hurried away.

Abigail walked to the front of the wagon, the oxen in their traces ready for the command to get moving. Her heart was heavy. Hollis would take it personally that some families didn't trust his leadership. It wasn't his fault that they'd been separated from the caravan.

Maybe she could've stopped him from saying what he had—or maybe not.

She knew how much he cared about getting this specific bunch of travelers across the mountains and to Oregon. And she knew—now—what he'd suffered in his past.

He hadn't meant to let her in, but that didn't change the fact that he needed help.

She didn't know what that would look like. Whether he would let her help or not. But someone needed to stand at Hollis's side. As a friend.

And perhaps that someone was supposed to be her. Even if he didn't want it to be.

* * *

Hollis's eyes scanned over the land ahead. A small bluff covered with a grove of trees extended on either side would provide a windbreak for the wagons when they circled in another forty-five minutes. A thread of relief flowed through him as he glanced down at the open logbook in his hand.

His mount shifted slightly beneath him, but Hollis moved easily with the horse.

The sun was on its downward trajectory. They'd made good time today, in spite of a handful of stops—once to dig a wagon out of a sandy spot and once to make a repair.

They'd make camp here. Hollis had a note in his book that nearby hunting should be viable.

Everything was fine. Only he felt discomfort, as if his experiences the past few days had turned him from a round peg that fit his role perfectly to a square block that no longer seemed to suit.

He wished he could forget the entire thing.

Pounding hoofbeats came from behind. He wheeled his horse, hand reaching to rest on the stock of his rifle.

Owen and August slowed their horses from a gallop. He worked to calm his pounding heart. Blew out a gusty exhale.

He was still too jumpy. Maybe because last night's sleep had been disjointed, a mix of memories and dreams.

He'd woken from a visceral dream of the kiss he'd shared with Abigail. The moment left him both ashamed and desperate to hold her again in his trembling arms.

"We'll camp here tonight," he said as Owen and August reined in and walked their horses toward him. He threw one arm wide to show the spot he'd imagined.

The men's gazes roamed the site for a moment, but then the two brothers shared a look before their attention returned to Hollis.

"What is it?" he prodded.

There'd been a long discussion this morning with the

captains—more questions than usual—about their route. What now?

"I rode back a piece," August said. "Looking for signs of the man you fought with."

The man's horse was lathered. Good thing the wagon train wasn't far behind. The animal could rest tonight. Hollis knew August wouldn't push him again tomorrow.

"There was no sign of any camp. I found the ridge you and Abigail climbed, found remnants of your big bonfire. But there was no sign of anyone else. No sign of a horse. Nothing." August's words were matter-of-fact, but the expression on his face was grim.

"The wildfire could've burned everything away," Hollis said. And with the heavy rains that had followed, it wouldn't be a surprise that any trace of hoof prints had washed away.

Owen's expression was carefully controlled. "You sure Abigail didn't get a look at the man? His horse? Anything?"

Hollis shook his head. "It was dark, smoke everywhere. She was too far away."

August's horse shifted. Hollis jerked his head, indicated for them to start moving. He'd go to meet the caravan and guide them to this campsite.

The brothers fell in beside each other on his left, all three of their horses at a walk.

"The Good Lord knows we've been watchful," Owen said.

The two men exchanged glances and then August spoke. "Owen was separated from camp and heard a rumor that someone was tracking the Fairfax women. Looking for an emerald."

The words spurred a memory from the depths of

Hollis's mind. Yes. He remembered Owen's fear when he'd returned to camp just over a week ago.

"We haven't seen any signs of a lone scout—or anyone," Owen said slowly. Thoughtfully? "Maybe he was a settler. Not someone following us."

"We'll want the men on watch, regardless," Hollis told him. He couldn't read Owen's stare. Did they think Hollis had made up the altercation?

"A few folks are feeling poorly," Owen offered next. "Upset stomachs, fever."

Hollis's stomach knotted. "We've had a few cases of something similar already," he said.

The Schaefer family had been hit by a stomach illness weeks ago. It'd affected Alice Spencer and a handful of others. There was always the worry of an epidemic. One big enough to spread throughout the caravan. But a few isolated cases didn't merit worry. Not yet.

The two brothers exchanged another glance. Hollis held back a sigh. Obviously, they needed to tell him something else. They'd ridden out here together when Owen could've come alone to make his report.

"What is it?" Hollis barked.

"There's been a lot of grousing today," Owen said. "Folks accusing you of being a hypocrite."

Hollis felt the sting of the words, fought to douse his temper when it threatened to spark. "In what way?"

Owen didn't look particularly happy to be the one delivering this news. "Some are saying you're a liar on account of not being married to Abigail. Some are saying you took liberties, being out there alone with a single woman for several days. And all that after you've held others to the company's rules."

Now his temper did ignite, but he bit back the roar that wanted to escape. What right did anyone have to talk about him like that? Or Abigail?

"Some of the women are saying its a scandal," August said quietly. "Getting their menfolk riled about having to follow your dictates when you are exempt."

For a blink, his memory pushed forward a slice of minutes when another company—Hollis's first trip across the prairie and mountains on the Oregon Trail—had bucked his leadership. He'd heard the whispers, one of his captains had mentioned the unrest.

He'd naively thought the trouble would blow over on its own. That his actions would speak louder than words, that they would see with their own eyes that his leadership was impeccable.

Instead, they'd formed a mob and attacked him. He'd been outnumbered, beaten. Lying on the ground, trying to protect his head even as a booted kick came flying toward his ribs. Through his arms, he could see snatches of the fear driving the travelers, fear turned into anger. Anger turned into a mob.

Abigail's brother, Joseph, had saved him. He'd stepped in with two other men and had run off the attackers.

The wagon train had split, with Hollis and a handful of wagons following his leadership. Only after they'd reached Oregon had he heard that the caravan that had split off from his company had suffered heavy losses—more than half their number had died along the journey.

"I'll make an announcement tonight," he said.

Owen frowned. "I'm not certain that's the best course."

Something tugged in Hollis's spirit at the argument.

He had to remind himself that Owen was a smart man, a good leader.

"What do you think should happen?" he prompted when Owen hesitated.

"They're not going to believe you, not when you can't refute that you said you and Abigail were married. And there's no hiding the fact that you were alone together for several days. If you were truly married, there'd be no talk."

Owen's words instantly conjured a vision—not a memory—of Abigail in a wedding dress, Abigail curled up against him in *their* bed.

He wanted that.

The want shamed him, so he shoved it away.

"No," he said sharply.

Owen's face turned into a storm cloud but August spoke gently, "If you'd consider—"

"I won't," Hollis interrupted.

"We could keep the ceremony quiet," Owen argued. "Pretend it'd happened before you two got lost. There were only a handful of folk who knew about me and Rachel in the beginning."

"She's already been in close company with you," August said quietly. "Always near Felicity, with you only a few wagons away."

"Because Joseph asked me to look after her."

The request had come in a letter along with fare for Abigail to make the journey from Independence. He'd owed Joseph, after the other man had saved his life. Hollis would've made a vow to the other man if he'd been present, instead he'd made a vow to himself to watch over Joseph's sister on the trail.

A vow that didn't include marrying her.

There was something broken inside Hollis. Joseph knew it. Marrying Abigail would be the last thing he would want.

"No." Hollis infused the word with finality. "I'll make an announcement tonight. Gather the captains—gather all the men once we're circled up and the oxen are cared for."

Owen's lips went tight, but he kicked his mount into a trot, quickly outpacing the other two. He glanced over his shoulder once, but August didn't move to join him.

Hollis kept his gaze resolutely over his horse's ears. He felt too raw to hear anything his scout had to say.

"Anything you need to talk about?"

Hollis shook his head at August's words.

"Clearly something happened between you and Abigail out there."

Hollis hated how calm his friend sounded, while Hollis's insides were twisting like a barrel of snakes.

"It's there in the way she looks at you."

A split-second flash of memory. Abigail's eyes, filled with affection and joy as she'd devoured the fish he'd grilled over the open fire.

"Nothing happened," Hollis growled.

August plodded along beside him for several quiet moments, then pushed his horse into a faster walk. Then he turned back and faced Hollis as Hollis kept his horse at a walk.

"Even if you make some kind of announcement, people are going to talk," August said. "About Abigail."

Hollis knew that. He hadn't been able to think about anything else since Owen had made his proclamation.

"Her reputation will be ruined. Word might even get out when we reach Oregon, if folks talk enough."

August wheeled his horse and rode off, dirt flying from beneath the horse's hooves, leaving Hollis to stew.

Ten lost. It had come to him that morning, a remembrance of the words' meaning.

Ten souls, lost on this journey.

So many.

If he didn't handle this correctly, if the wagon train split, there was a chance more folks would die out here.

He had a responsibility to the company.

And a responsibility to Abigail.

She'd be affected if people speculated about their relationship, about what might've happened between them during those days they were alone together. He couldn't damage her prospects for a good marriage in Oregon.

Something inside of him revolted at the idea of her married to another man. Yet she would never have that chance if he let the rumors fly. She'd be ruined.

But if he agreed to a foolhardy marriage, he'd ruin himself.

Ten

"YOUR PATIENT NEEDS to drink fresh milk every day," Doc said.

Maddie Fairfax looked up from where she knelt in a patch of what looked like green weeds, a flash of surprise and... dismay crossing her expressive features.

Good. Then they were both dismayed. He didn't want to be out here having this conversation.

He'd followed her from camp, keeping his distance. When she'd disappeared in the woods, he'd walked faster. For a moment he worried he'd lost her completely. Like she was some kind of wood sprite sent to steal him away from the caravan.

"Are you speaking of Mrs. Bouye? Where do you suggest she finds a milk cow?" She gestured expansively to the woods and prairie surrounding them, almost knocking over the woven basket at her side.

She did not ask how he'd found out that her eight-months pregnant patient was complaining of her teeth aching. Which meant he didn't have to tell her that he was

135

constantly spying, listening for hints of conversations that mentioned her.

It wasn't about her at all. It was about the folks on this wagon train receiving adequate medical care. Where did he expect this woman to find a cow? Her question prodded him.

"We're nearing the fort in a day or two," he reminded Maddie, who'd gone back to threading her delicate fingers through the fronds of a green fern before she plucked something from its base. "Your patient should purchase a milk cow there."

"She and her husband don't have the money for that," she muttered as she kept on with her task. "These herbs will help."

"The herbs are not enough," he ground out.

She slowly rose to her feet, the movement graceful. He wanted to look away.

He wanted to watch her forever.

Her eyes flashed at him before he'd even blinked. "You can't fix everything. Not out here. Surely you know that."

"Of course I do." Doc was peripherally aware of a young voice calling out, "Doc!" but he couldn't seem to break the stare he was caught in.

Maddie was pink-cheeked, determination narrowing her eyes. A fire inside her that somehow matched his own. As he witnessed her temper spark, he couldn't keep his eyes from dropping to the stubborn set of her lips.

His chest felt tight, like he suffered from a breathing complaint and couldn't catch his breath.

She was—

"Doc!" The young voice was closer now. Maddie was

the one who broke the stare first, her attention moving behind Doc.

Blood pounded in his temples as he turned, now aware of someone crashing through the undergrowth.

Young Alex appeared, red-faced and out of breath.

Doc was both relieved and angry at the interruption. He meant to convince Maddie that her care for the pregnant woman was *wrong*—

"I need ya," Alex gasped as he ran up. "You put in those stitches an' your bandage ain't broke—" The boy broke off his rattled sentence to gulp in a breath. He must've run all the way out here.

Doc was aware that Maddie had knelt back on the ground, foraging again.

"Another animal friend?" There was an impatience to his tone but the boy didn't seem to hear it.

Alex shook his head. "No, it's—can we hurry?"

Doc didn't particularly desire to patch up another in the menagerie he'd been shown three days ago after stitching up the boy's dog.

"Don't you want..." Doc turned slightly as he gestured to Maddie.

Her head came up, and he saw the judgment in her eyes. He knew exactly what she was thinking. "He asked for you," she said in a low voice.

"Doc, it's my sis! She's bleedin' everywhere."

It only took a second to register that what Doc had taken for excitement was fear and that the boy was trembling and gasping with urgency.

Alex had his full attention now.

He started running, the boy beside him. Aware of

Maddie abandoning her basket and lifting her skirts to run, too.

"What happened?" he demanded.

"Ma told my brother to watch Jenny, but Pa told him to fetch his bridle. I was over by the fire. Paul put Jenny in the wagon, but she fell out!"

That could mean any number of injuries. He'd said earlier that she was bleeding. Had she cut herself? Broken her arm so badly that the bone was protruding?

The wagons in sight, the boy let out a sob.

"Which way?" Doc asked.

The boy bent over and retched, clearly out of breath and worked up from what he'd witnessed and his wild run to find Doc.

"This way," Maddie urged. "Catch up to us," she called back to the boy.

For a breath, he was grateful that she knew where she was going. He spared a moment to ask Alex to fetch his doctor's bag from his horse.

He could hear the pained screams before they reached the circle of wagons.

"How old?" he asked Maddie.

She was breathing as hard as he was, chest heaving. "Not yet two."

That would make things more difficult. A child that age couldn't tell them where it hurt.

Moments later, they slowed and approached two other women, mothers he recognized from the company. They seemed relieved to see him—or possibly Maddie—and faded into the background, revealing a young man no older than thirteen holding one hand over a squirming toddler's cheek. Blood trailed down his arm, was smeared over her face.

The little one slapped at her brother's hold, trailing blood farther.

The young man—Paul?—was crying.

"Miss Maddie, ya gotta help!" he said.

"Let me," Doc said as he shouldered Maddie out of the way. He reached out for the girl. "Be still now."

But the wailing babe screamed louder and struggled against him when he tried to hold her.

"I got yer bag." Alex ran up, extending the black leather bag toward Doc. He bobbled it and almost dropped it.

"Be careful," Doc barked. There were medicine bottles inside, and if one got crushed, precious remedies would be lost.

"Put it down," he told the boy, who looked frozen, tears welling in his eyes.

Urgency pressed, but it was Maddie coming in just behind Doc's elbow that discombobulated everything. She touched Alex's shoulder, gently pried the bag from his fingers. "Can you add wood to the fire? We need some hot water."

The boy took a deep breath under her gentle command and nodded, steadying himself, rushing to do what she'd asked.

Jenny was still wailing and screaming.

Maddie pressed the bag into Doc's stomach with more force than was necessary. Her eyes flashed at him, devoid of the compassion she'd just shared with the boy.

"Perhaps you'd have more patients if your bedside manner improved," she whispered fiercely.

By the time she'd turned back to the preteen and his young sister, she was all smiles.

"That was scary, wasn't it?" she cooed. She brushed damp hair back from the baby's forehead, her fingers quick and gentle.

She glanced over her shoulder, asking him whether he'd seen the start of a jagged cut near the little one's eyebrow. The rest of the gash was covered over with the older boy's hand.

"Did someone fetch your mother?" This time Maddie's gentle touch went to Paul's shoulder.

He took a shuddering breath, and then Doc saw him visibly calm.

In the span of several heartbeats, she'd calmed all three children. The girl was still crying, but her wailing and screaming had stopped.

"Do you want to come to me?" Maddie asked. With one hand on the girl's back, she reached out her other arm.

The girl went easily into her arms.

Doc inhaled, ready to argue why he should be the one to tend to her wound, but Maddie had already turned in his direction, gently brushing more of the girl's hair out of her face.

"I'm going to sit," she murmured, and then perched on a crate only steps away before waving him over. He joined them, on his knees in front of the little girl, who turned her face into Maddie's neck.

Blood streaked Maddie's jaw and beneath her ear, but she didn't flinch.

"What's her name?" he murmured.

"Jenny," Maddie reminded him gently. "Jenny, this is Doc Jason. He's the one who fixed up Tommy, remember?"

Doc Jason.

He didn't have time for her use of his name to pinch. But he still felt it.

The girl peeked at him with one eye.

In a matter of moments, Maddie had distracted her by helping her clean off a small scrape on her knee. Doc wiped clean the cut that began at her eyebrow and extended down to her cheek. The brothers brought clean rags and hot water and soon enough Doc was ready to start putting in the stitches.

He didn't have to tell Maddie to keep Jenny still. She was singing a song, the brogue in her voice stronger. She gently clasped the girl's wrists in one hand while her other arm banded around Jenny's middle.

He tried not to notice, tried to keep his focus entirely on the small, neat stitches. But he couldn't help seeing Maddie lay her cheek gently against Jenny's hair. How the soft brushes of her fingertips over the girl's skin soothed her. Maddie's voice echoed through his head.

Jenny's mother rushed into camp as he sewed the last stitch, her hair hung wet down her back, eyes frantic.

The woman immediately calmed when she saw Maddie had her daughter. The two boys circled around their ma, talking as fast as possible.

Doc moved away from Maddie and Jenny, using the moment to look for a bandage at the bottom of his bag.

He couldn't help the glance that snuck back toward her.

She was smiling, playing a version of one-handed pat-a-cake with the girl.

She would make a good mother.

The tension inside of him rolled to a boil and he had to

turn away. She looked so *young*. With her entire life ahead of her.

She was a reminder of everything he'd lost.

And everything he'd never have again.

* * *

"She pretended to be an upstanding woman, but now Ma says she's not. She's like a soiled dove from one of those saloons."

"Who'd ever want to marry someone like that?"

Hollis rounded a campfire where two teen girls hadn't bothered to keep their voices down. One of the two wore a tightly-braided mass of black curls that reminded Hollis of his mother.

The sun was on its descent and the last of the wagons were circling up. Several of the first wagons had already unloaded, and he was on his way to see Abigail.

It would be another hour before the group met for his announcement, and he still wasn't sure what he was going to say to the company. And now this.

The girl with braids caught sight of him and the thundercloud that must be his expression, because she ducked her head meekly. Her companion was facing away from him when he passed by their supper preparations.

She gestured with one hand. "My ma was worried things out here in the west would be uncouth."

The first teen nudged her friend with an elbow. The girl looked around, and her eyes went wide.

"Evening, Mr. Hollis." The girl with the braids almost gasped the words.

He should stop and speak to them. They were clearly talking about Abigail, spreading gossip. Anger surged through his veins. Abigail had helped a dozen families throughout their time on the Trail. Maybe more. She'd worked tirelessly to feed folks when they were ill, to help with chores. To triage and help Maddie doctor folks when the tornado had wrecked their company, when the outlaws had attacked.

She didn't deserve this.

And he was the only one who could do anything about it.

He passed by with a grimace instead of a smile and hoped they'd think twice about their talk.

He still wasn't sure of his words when he found Abigail crouched over a fire she must've only just lit. She was feeding twigs from a small supply to grow the flames.

I know this.

For a moment, the memory of her looking up at him with shining eyes from that primitive bow drill blasted through his mind like a stampeding buffalo.

He cleared his throat. "We need to talk."

When she glanced up, her eyes were hooded. "Supper will be ready soon. If you're famished now, I've got some biscuits left from breakfast." Her lashes fluttered down, hiding her gaze from him.

Something tugged deep inside, a wish that he didn't dare admit to.

"I'll eat later," he said.

This time, the look she gave him was pointed. "You've got to keep your strength up." Her eyes softened. "That scrape on your face looks a mite better."

She shifted her attention back to the fire, as if she

couldn't bear to look at him for longer. The fire popped, but she didn't jump.

Her words made his chest ache. When was the last time someone had worried whether he'd eaten enough, or that his wounds were healing? Probably his Ma, before he'd left home.

Years ago, he'd told his family he was coming west. He'd had letters from home, but had never written back. Just this spring, he'd received a letter from his brother Booker that he wanted to take the Oregon Trail. But Hollis had left before Booker arrived in Independence.

He hadn't let anyone close enough to care whether he was all right. Not since Dinah had passed away.

"Aren't you angry at me?" He scratched the back of his neck. "You've probably got a right to it after the way I talked to you last night."

There was a prolonged moment where she kept her face averted before she stood, swiping dust off her hands. When she finally glanced at him, her eyes were clear. "No matter what, I hope we're still friends."

Her words threaded hope through the tightness in his chest. Hope he didn't deserve.

But she wasn't done. "I think you need a friend."

Her words left him breathless. He forced down the jolt of affection and warmth her words conjured. Best to shut that down. Or ignore it, if he could.

He let his stare on her harden. "I'm sure you've heard the talk around camp."

A shadow flickered behind her eyes, the minute clasp and release of her hand into a fist at her side.

"I don't want your reputation sullied."

A flash of fire lit her eyes now and a stubbornness lifted her chin. "That's not your problem to worry about."

She moved to the lowered tailgate of her wagon and began pulling things toward her. A large crock. A wooden spoon.

The stubborn woman might not admit it, but she was his responsibility as part of the wagon train. And that included her reputation.

He took two steps closer, took another look around to make sure no one was within listening distance. "It is my problem if I say it is."

She didn't look at him, but he saw the way her lips tightened.

"We should get married," he blurted.

He'd had a different plan in mind, a formal announcement to the company that had been running through his brain since August and Owen had come to him. But he couldn't keep fighting against common sense. And neither should she.

She'd gone still at his words, frozen in place. Now, as she turned toward him, he couldn't bear to see questions in her eyes. Or whatever else he might find there.

It was his turn to avert his face, to pretend he was looking at oxen being led to a nearby stream. "It'll be a marriage in name only," he said stiffly.

A way to protect her. The only way he could figure. August had been right. "Once we get to Oregon, we'll have it annulled and go our separate ways."

She was quiet. Abigail, who had once confronted him with August about his memory problems. Who'd forced him to eat when he'd been poorly.

He steeled himself and arranged his expression to

careful emptiness when he looked at her. "It won't mean anything," he said dispassionately. "Not even friendship. When we reach Oregon, it'll be over."

She was watching him with tear-filled eyes that probably saw too much. He'd told her about Dinah when no one else knew.

"Fine." Her agreement was quiet. Determined. But her lower lip quivered and she averted her face.

His stomach twisted. He was doing this to *protect* her. Not to hurt her. He had to know. "No arguments?"

She shook her head slightly, still not looking at him. Went back to her cooking. After a quiet moment, she began humming under her breath. Had she really settled the matter in her mind that quickly?

His shirt collar felt like it was choking him, like he couldn't draw a full breath.

"Stay here. I'll fetch Owen to do the honors," he muttered before he stalked off.

Owen showed a rare reaction—relief flitting across his expression—when Hollis fetched him. Hollis pushed his prayer book into the other man's hands. "Let's go."

Owen only trailed him for a step, then fell in beside him. "You'll have to move your bedroll, camp together," he said.

"I know," Hollis snapped.

He'd barely come to terms with what he'd agreed to. He'd deal with the forced closeness when it was time.

Abigail was waiting for them, her meal ready to be put on the fire but covered with a cloth.

Hollis didn't want any eyes on them. Not for this. This was between him and Abigail. He marched out in front of

Owen and Abigail until they were out of eyesight and earshot from camp. Awareness of how quickly the camp announcement would be upon him rankled his nerves.

Facing Abigail made Hollis's insides knot.

Owen started reading from the page Hollis had marked. Hollis had said the words enough times that they flowed over him like water.

He tried to ignore the way Abigail watched him, her expression grave, eyes big in her face. Tried to recall Dinah and the speaking of their own vows, tried to pull her into this moment, overlay Abigail's face with Dinah's.

But his past was fuzzy and vague and when he blinked, Abigail filled his vision.

She was the one sharing this moment with him, the one whose fingers trembled in his when Owen made them clasp hands. Or maybe that was him shaking.

Was this a mistake? Was he making everything worse?

Her grip steadied him, gave an anchor when he felt as if a stiff breeze would be able to knock him over.

She spoke her vows in a clear voice, her eyes shining with promise.

That wasn't what they'd agreed to, a voice inside him shouted. This was a farce! It wasn't real! But when it was time for him to speak his own vows, the words were full of an unexpected gravity.

He wrestled with his feelings, forcing the twisting thing inside him to agree that this was all to protect Abigail. He'd keep her close, physically, just to make sure the gossip didn't touch her, and he could deliver her safely to Joseph.

Hollis would keep the walls in his heart sturdy and secure. He wouldn't share himself with her the way he had while they'd been lost to the wilderness. He couldn't afford to care.

"You'd better kiss her to make it official," Owen muttered.

Hollis's heart jerked in his chest. He hadn't thought of this complication.

Then Abigail reached up on tiptoe and kissed the corner of his mouth. Her hand was a brand as it touched his cheek and then was gone.

"I'll fetch you before I meet with the men." Was that his voice, the gravel-filled grunt?

"I'll be ready."

* * *

"I'll be ready." Abigail had said the words, but she didn't feel ready when Hollis returned to find her a scant handful of minutes later. She was shaken. In disbelief.

She'd married Hollis.

But it wasn't an occasion for celebration. It was grief that filled her. Grief over a loveless marriage.

He didn't speak to her, only offered his arm in silence. She took it, aware of the strength in his muscled forearm beneath her fingertips, the brush of her shoulder against his biceps.

I take thee, Abigail, to be my wedded wife.

She'd seen the pure panic in Hollis's eyes, everything else in his expression frozen as he'd repeated the words Owen prompted. He didn't want this marriage. She'd known it from the way he'd offered to marry her.

But she'd also spoken true. He needed a friend. Needed

a helpmeet. And she could be that for him. Even if it wouldn't last past the end of their journey.

I take thee, Hollis, to be my wedded husband.

She'd meant the vows she'd spoken before Hollis and Owen and the Lord. She couldn't say when it had happened—though definitely before they'd been lost to the raging river—but she'd begun to care deeply for Hollis, for the man who held himself apart. Who cared for every single person, no matter how big or how small, on this wagon train. Who pushed himself harder than anyone else.

But she had no expectation that he'd ever return her feelings. She would never forget the expression on his face when he'd told her he'd lost his wife.

Hollis was a man who loved deeply. No doubt his wife had been someone terribly special. Someone he'd chosen, not been forced to marry.

Abigail would never compare to her. She didn't dare try.

But she could still help him.

As they passed through the camp, she caught curious, wide-eyed gazes from several of the women corralling children and preparing supper.

Hollis remained stoic, focused. His mind probably on addressing the men. It was left to Abigail to smile gently, to pretend that it didn't hurt that these women thought she was immoral. She knew the truth.

She was surprised to see Leo, Evangeline, Owen and Rachel waiting near an empty crate. She'd seen Hollis stand on one before to address the crowd of men all around.

"I thought you might need some support," he murmured to her so low that no one else could hear.

The nerves that had been jangling as they'd walked began to settle as warmth trickled into her chest. Evangeline smiled, but Rachel sent a pointed look to Abigail's hand on Hollis's arm. When he let go of her and stepped up onto the crate, the women flanked her, their husbands standing just behind.

Hollis let out a shrill whistle that quieted the murmuring crowd.

"I understand there's been some restlessness in camp while I was away." His voice boomed out over the settlers and the empty prairie around them as stars began to peek out from the velvety blue sky. A few men at the front of the crowd cast sheepish looks toward the ground.

"That's not surprising around this time on our journey. Supplies start to dwindle. Wagons break. Things get difficult."

Abigail saw the nodding heads, the way some of the men listened intently. Hollis was wise to remind everyone that he'd done this twice before. That he knew what they were experiencing.

"The worst thing that can happen to a company is for complaining voices and gossip to bring division."

Beaumont, toward the front of the crowd, frowned. He muttered something to his neighbor, but Hollis didn't seem to notice the small moment of dissent.

"There were a lot of wagon masters you could have chosen in Independence. You chose to travel with me for a reason." *This* man, this leader was determined and confident. "I haven't told you this story, but maybe I should've before we pulled out. On my first overland journey, our company split because of some differences of opinion. The part of our company that left suffered great losses—more than half of them didn't make it to Oregon alive. The company I led lost two." He spoke the words seriously, without an ounce of bragging in his tone.

She shivered. She knew how much those losses would have affected him. Some of the men glanced nervously at their neighbors.

"Before we left, you gave me your trust. I ask that you remember why you came to me in Independence. Why you wanted to travel with this company and not on your own. I will get you to Oregon as safely as I can."

He earned several nods, but she couldn't look away from his face. This Hollis was charismatic, a born leader. Who wouldn't follow him?

"Some of them don't seem convinced," Leo murmured from somewhere behind her in a voice so low she barely heard it.

Owen grunted. Agreement?

"There's also been some speculation about my personal life and that of one of our fellow travelers."

Her face flamed as several gazes landed on her. Her heart pounded and her palms went sweaty.

"Breathe," Evangeline whispered.

Hollis glanced over at her, and she recognized affection in his expression. He continued to address the crowd. "As far as I'm concerned, our private lives are our own business, but if it will settle your minds, I'd like to introduce my wife, Abigail."

He extended a hand toward her.

Leo and Owen clapped heartily. A few of the crowd joined in, at first awkward and slow until a spatter of applause spread through the rest.

Abigail had only seen this warmth in Hollis's eyes

when his memory had been gone. She knew it wasn't real, that it was for the benefit of the crowd, but she beamed back at him. That's what he wanted, wasn't it?

"I'm certain I don't need to remind you how indispensable my wife has been thus far on our journey. She's doctored many of you, helped your wives when they had a sick child to care for, shared her own food supplies. Her optimistic spirit is unmatched in this company. I know you can all understand why I fell for Abigail."

Her insides knotted as his statements followed one after another. She understood his reasoning, but she knew the truth, too. She fretted and worried as much as anyone else. But Hollis made her sound hopeful and bright.

He continued speaking, telling the men that they'd reach the nearest fort in a few days.

As he wrapped up and the gathering began to disperse, Evangeline gave Abigail a hug. "You'll be good for him!" she whispered in Abigail's ear.

Rachel must have overheard. Her brows pinched slightly in concern. "Let me know if I can help in any way," was her whisper.

Most of the company, Evangeline and Leo included, believed their union to be real. But perhaps Rachel had guessed the truth.

"Our nearest neighbors have a sick little boy," Evangeline said. "I thought to check on them. Perhaps you'd like to come with me?"

Abigail became aware of Hollis at her elbow. "Abigail and I can check on them together."

His expression was serious as he scanned the groups of men dispersing to their families.

"And then you'll eat dinner," Abigail murmured.

"Already a haranguing wife," Owen teased, though his eyes held a serious glint.

Evangeline and Leo chuckled.

Hollis excused them.

In a nearby camp, the mother and child were pale and complained of stomachaches. Abigail offered to bring them some broth as soon as she could. She made small talk for several moments while Hollis spoke to the woman's husband.

As they left, walking together toward her cookfire, she asked, "Is there anything to be worried about?"

He shook his head. "I don't think so. Husband said they'd drank water straight from the river after the flooding. Who knows what could've been stirred up in it. It'll likely pass in its own time."

His mind was clearly on something else, his eyes vacant and words distracted.

When someone called out to him, his eyes glittered as he leaned in close, brushing his nose to her cheek—pretending to kiss her goodbye?

"Don't forget your supper," she called after him.

He waved over his shoulder.

Only as she reached camp and focused on her tasks did she let loose of the tight rein she'd kept on her emotions since the moment Hollis had said, "We should get married."

With her head ducked over the cooking pot, she could admit to what she didn't dare breathe to anyone: she wished it was real.

The marriage.

The way he looked at her.

She'd seen what no one else seemed to be able to see.

The lines around his eyes, the weight of responsibility he carried for the company.

She knew him.

Knew she shouldn't hope.

He'd loved his Dinah dearly. There was no room in his heart for Abigail.

Eleven

ABIGAIL AWAKENED when the man in the bedroll next to hers stirred.

She came to awareness instantly, but kept her eyes closed.

Hollis.

Their wedding ceremony.

Him presenting her to the company as his wife.

He stirred again, the fabric of his clothes shifting against his bedroll.

She peeked her eyes open. It was early morning, but still dark. The sun hadn't come up.

The campfire that had burned last night several feet in front of her now pulsed dully with its last warm coals. It needed stirring, and feeding, if she was to keep it going for breakfast.

Behind her, she could sense Hollis sitting up in his bedroll with a deep, sleepy inhale.

For a moment, she squeezed her eyes closed again, wanting his arm around her.

The wagon was behind him, their camp on the front edge of the company. When the wagons left their circle later this morning, hers would be second in line.

At another movement behind her, she sat up, working to untangle her feet from the bedroll.

"I didn't mean to wake you," Hollis whispered, his breath on her jaw. He must've bent close to say the words so quietly.

By the time she glanced up, he'd scooted back, a larger shadow against the darkness.

"How late did you come to bed?" she whispered, keenly aware of other travelers only yards away, still asleep. One loud snore possibly belonged to their neighbor, Mr. Schaefer.

She'd lain awake for a long time after the camp had quieted, children's voices had faded, movement had stopped, fires had slowly burned down. She didn't know what time she'd finally drifted off, only that it'd been far past the time when Hollis should've been abed.

His hesitation before he returned a quiet, "Late," told her more than the word itself.

Had he delayed his rest simply because of the arrangement of their bedrolls?

The cool morning air chilled her exposed arms and she drew her shawl out of the bedroll—a trick she'd learned early on the journey, one meant to bring the warmth of her bedroll into the chilly spring mornings—and slipped it around her shoulders.

As she pulled on her boots and made to stand, Hollis protested, "It's early yet. Stay abed."

She shook her head, even though he couldn't see it, and whispered, "I'm already up."

They must've both thought to stir the fire, because she bumped into his brawny shoulder as she crossed right and he moved left. One big hand steadied her waist, dropping away quickly as if the touch had burned him.

After being momentarily frozen, he moved past her to squat near the ashes and embers. One stir with a long stick and hot coals were unearthed, sending warm light to illuminate his stony expression.

She fetched the coffeepot from the back of the wagon, where she'd left it filled with water and ready for the morning.

He'd grown the fire to a small flame that licked and crackled with each new twig he fed it. She joined him at the fire, earning a there-and-gone glance before he returned his attention to the flames. She held the coffeepot, waiting for the fire to burn bigger.

"How are your ribs?" she asked quietly.

A flash of surprise crossed his face, quickly hidden. He twisted his torso in both directions, widening his shoulders and opening his chest as he did. She saw only a tiny tightening of his mouth when he twisted to the left.

"Better. Bruises fading."

The fire was hot enough to start the coffee, so she nudged the pot into the coals at its edge. She was determined to have his breakfast finished before he left camp this morning. She returned to the wagon to mix up another pan of biscuits and rubbed one hand over her cheek in frustration.

"Something the matter?"

She jumped at Hollis's voice from just beside her. She hadn't realized he had come to join her.

"I'm tired of biscuits," she admitted.

"Me too." It was too dark here, with her back turned to the fire, but she imagined that the tenor of his voice meant he'd smiled with one corner of his mouth.

He reached for something inside the wagon. It must've been out of reach, because his side bumped her arm as he shifted, grunted, and strained to get whatever it was he was after. When he moved, he turned, but he turned toward her instead of away, so that her shoulders brushed his chest.

For a single moment, they stayed like that. Close enough that she could smell the soap he must've washed with last night, the man beneath. Close enough that he could tip her chin up—with an abrupt movement, he left, cool air flowing in to the space he'd vacated.

She'd known things would be different between them, especially with the marriage forcing them into closer proximity. But she hadn't expected it would feel so awkward.

If she was feeling this way, he had to be as well. Her thoughts spun as she mixed the biscuits in the dark, formed the dough by touch, wiped sticky fingers on a cloth. When she returned to the fire, he had his logbook tipped toward the flames, using the scant light to read.

She slid the pan of biscuits on a tripod in the fire, where they'd cook, careful to keep her skirts out of the way of a flying spark.

The coffee had warmed, and she carefully poured a cup, moving around the fire to offer it to Hollis. The earthy scent must've overcome his hesitation because he took it with a murmured, "Thank you."

She sat where she could attend the biscuits and watched him in the firelight. The quiet all around them made their interactions seem more intimate.

He glanced up and caught her looking. Stuck one finger in his book. "What?"

"Was... was losing your wife the reason you started leading wagon trains west?"

She'd been wondering ever since he'd revealed his past. She'd lost a parent, but not a spouse. Surely that grief had to run even deeper. Was that what'd sent him on this journey?

"In a way." He stared at the fire.

She was surprised he'd answered her impertinent question.

"After I lost Dinah and the baby, *I* was lost."

Dinah. Hearing the name knotted Abigail's stomach.

"I couldn't stay in the house where we'd lived. Memories of her haunted every room. Every single thing inside of it was full of pain."

She understood that. She'd been grateful for the job after her mam had passed, but being in the same kitchen where they'd worked side by side was like working with a ghost. She couldn't count the times she'd turned with a word on her lips for her mam. Almost with the shadow of mam in the corner of her eye.

And then she'd remember. Mam was gone. And every time brought a new cut of grief.

"I read a newspaper article about the Oregon Trail, the need for men to guide families along the route. So I came."

There was more behind his words. She was sure of it. "But why not settle?" she pressed. "Why do you keep on?"

He was slow to reply, his words measured and thoughtful. "Making the journey is like a part of my past that keeps calling me. When I was very young, my pa and ma took me and left—they escaped from a slaveholder and ran to the north. I only have snatches of memories from the journey. All that way on foot, with nothing to their names," he shook his head, eyes distant. "My pa never spoke of it, but sometimes, even when I was grown, he'd watch over his shoulder with a haunted expression." He shifted slightly. "The only things I remember are running down a dirt-packed road in the night and a belly so empty, a hunger so deep—"

He snapped himself out of the memory and sipped his coffee. "Part of me still carries that. Will always carry those memories."

A silence unfolded as his story settled between them. He'd shared not only the words, but a deeper vulnerability. She barely breathed, not wanting to ruin the moment.

He went on, "I didn't plan on taking the journey more than once. But I realized folks needed someone and that I could do it."

"You're a good leader." The praise slipped past her lips easily, because it was true.

His eyes went downcast and he hid his face behind another sip of coffee.

Another question had been wearing at her ever since he'd mentioned his late wife.

"What was she like?" she whispered, unsure she actually wanted to hear the answer.

He stared over the fire now, his gaze far off. "She was... stately. There was a refinement about her, no matter what menial task she might be doing." His voice went husky as he spoke these words.

Abigail glanced at her palms in the flickering firelight. She certainly wasn't elegant. She had the hands of someone who worked in the kitchen—calloused, with scars from nicks that'd healed over and old burns.

As if he'd noticed her looking, Hollis said, "She had her own scars. She came from a free family, but they'd been driven out of the town where she'd grown up. There was a mark, just here." He indicated a spot at the left side of his jaw. "She'd been struck by a rock thrown by a man who hated her family simply for the color of their skin." He blinked, and tipped his head. "You've never met a woman so determined." His eyes flashed to Abigail and away again. He went quiet.

"My mam was like that," Abigail shared. She smoothed invisible lines in her skirt as the sun began to lighten the sky. "Determined. She taught me to keep on, keep smiling. Keep singing. Even when she was sacked without cause, she kept singing."

The first silver from the rising sun crested the horizon and Abigail blinked in the light, hiding the moisture of unexpected tears. She sensed Hollis watching her and averted her face as she knelt on the ground near the fire. She used her apron to protect her hand as she pulled the biscuit tin from the fire. She'd overcooked one side. They were dark brown instead of pale gold.

Abigail remembered Hollis's words when he'd announced to the company that she was his wife. He'd called her optimistic. But Abigail wasn't like Mam. Abigail's joyful spirit was a mask. Every moment out here in the wild was a moment of fear. Fear that she'd lose everything she held dear. But she couldn't admit that to him.

"I think Dinah would've liked you," he said quietly.

When she straightened from the fire, he had already ducked his head.

Her stomach twisted. Dinah would've liked her. But Hollis didn't.

She went to the wagon to plate some of the biscuits for Hollis, grateful for the moment to turn her back. She was the one who'd prompted the conversation, asked about his wife. But she hadn't expected to feel the well of emptiness that came with the discovery of how deeply Hollis had loved her.

* * *

Hollis ate the biscuits, part of him realizing the delicious taste while the bigger part of him tasted only ash. He tracked August as the man walked into the circle of wagons after a shift on watch.

August caught his stare and shook his head. Still no sign of any man riding alone.

Disappointment surged. Hollis wished he could *know* whether the man he'd met in the wildfire and storm had been following the company. Or had he been a lone traveler, worried for his own survival? It bothered Hollis that no one else had seen any sign of him.

A few others from the company were stirring, but most of the camp slept on. The sun was rising over the eastern horizon, a ball of fire. Folks were tired. They needed the rest, though Hollis hoped to make twenty miles today.

Abigail puttered around the wagon, keeping her back to him. He felt like his insides were on fire. He hadn't realized until he'd dredged up the memories how much he'd forgotten about Dinah. The loss felt fresh all over again. Five years ago, he'd forced himself to forget, pushing through the dangerous overland journeys, working like a dog until all he could do was drop into his bedroll at night. Too tired to cry, to face the grief that had dogged his every step.

Now he couldn't find a clear memory of Dinah's smile. Every time he pushed, his traitorous mind brought a flash of Abigail's wide, happy grin and bright eyes.

Grief flared, hot and bright. He'd longed to have that family with Dinah. Longed for their baby to arrive, not knowing that would be the end of everything good for him. After awhile, he couldn't face his parents, the shared grief too much to bear.

Abigail moved behind the wagon. He still felt the awkwardness of waking up next to her—of bumping into her in the semi-darkness. In camp, everything was different from their mornings together in the wild.

He wanted to pull her closer, wanted her in his arms again.

He wanted to be across camp. Away from her.

Now was his chance. The sun was up, which meant he could get to work.

He returned the tin plate she'd given him to the wagon. She was tying off a strap where one of the pails hung along side.

"Better'n my ma's biscuits," he said. "Thank you."

She glanced his way in surprise. "Is your mother still living?"

He swallowed a sudden hot knot in his throat at the mention of his mama and nodded. "Far as I know. My pa owns a livery back East. My brothers and sister live there too. Or they did when I first came West. One of my brothers might've come West."

Her brows crinkled. "You don't know?" A hint of censure in her voice.

"I left before he reached Independence."

There was a bit of judgment in the sideways glance she sent him. "I can't wait to see Joseph. It's difficult when letters take forever to find each other—or they don't at all."

"I haven't written them since I left." Why had he admitted that?

Her sharp look was an echo of the guilt he felt.

"Whyever not?"

It was too difficult to find the words. To admit out loud to something he'd only admitted to himself. Especially to someone as joyful as Abigail.

"I've known for a long time that I'll end up alone." It was easier to say it if he didn't look at her, so he didn't. It was better that she knew why they couldn't make a real go of this marriage.

He watched the horizon, watched a little jut of rocks where a hill rose in the distance. And he caught sight of a glint of light.

Something man-made. It couldn't be natural, the flash, pause, flash of light.

The sun was reflecting off of a pair of field glasses.

His body reacted before he could think anything through. He left Abigail without a word, heading for his horse picketed outside the line of wagons. He didn't take his eyes off that place against the hill, though the flashing had stopped.

There was someone out there. Maybe the same man who'd attacked him.

His heart raced, pulse pounding in his temples as he quickly saddled his horse and put on the bridle. He made sure his rifle was strapped into place, felt for the gun belt at his side.

Whoever was out there had been looking straight toward their camp. There couldn't be any good reason for that. Why not approach the wagon train and state your business?

Unless your business was nefarious.

Finally in the saddle, Hollis took off. The man who'd attacked him wouldn't get a second chance. It wasn't a matter of pride. Hollis had the wagon train to protect.

He kept his eyes wide open, one hand on his rifle stock, and slowed his horse as he neared the place the flash had come from. Dark rocks rose from the prairie, and bushes and brush would give a man ample places to hide. Awareness sent gooseflesh skittering up the back of his neck, but even when he strained his ears, Hollis couldn't hear a sound other than his own harsh breaths.

Where had the man gone?

He searched for several minutes, until a familiar voice hailed, "Hollis!"

Owen approached on horseback from the same direction Hollis had come. The sun was up now, faint, high clouds scuttling across the sky with the dry wind. Easy enough to see his captain's frown as his horse picked its way over the terrain.

When Owen was close, Hollis, still on his horse, pointed to a mark in a sandy drift. "That look like a hoof print to you?"

Owen squinted. "Maybe?" His frown grew as his eyes scanned Hollis. "What're you doing out here?"

He sounded almost accusing. Hollis bristled. "I saw light flashing. Reflecting off field glasses, most like."

Owen glanced around, eyes skeptical. "You sure about that?"

Hollis didn't know why the man questioned him. He didn't have time for games. The company needed to move out soon, and he needed to find whoever'd been out here. But when he tried to move his horse, Owen blocked him with his mount.

"Move," Hollis ordered.

"Abigail told me you high-tailed it outta camp awhile ago. You find any sign of anyone out here?"

Hollis didn't have to answer to Owen. *He* was the wagonmaster. He narrowed his eyes at his captain. "Is there something you want to say?"

"We need your leadership in camp." Owen said the words with a tightness to his jaw. "You're distracted."

There was something else there, something he wasn't saying. Hollis's horse sidestepped, sensitive to the tension between the two men.

"Ever since you and Abigail got back, you've been preoccupied."

Did he mean by Abigail? "You're the one who pushed for me to marry her," he growled.

Things would be a lot less muddled if Abigail wasn't in the mix.

"It's more than that," Owen said. Color had risen high in his cheeks, and Hollis felt his own temper flare.

"You need to say something, say it," Hollis said.

"August told me there were holes in your memory before you and Abigail got washed away in the river."

The words battered Hollis like a blow. The head injury he'd received when the twister had struck had far-reaching repercussions—one of which was Hollis's short term memory that'd been hit or miss.

It hadn't bothered him since he and Abigail had woken up from those poisonous berries. He hadn't even had to think about it. But August had remembered what Hollis had told him in confidence—though he'd had no choice. And August had told his brother.

Betrayal sparked Hollis's temper to a flame.

"My memory is fine now." He gritted out the words.

"Is it?" Owen challenged. "Because two days ago, August went back to where you claimed to be attacked and there was nothing there. Now this," he gestured around them. "There's nothing here. You imagined those flashes out here."

Behind the betrayal and anger burning a hole in his gut was a tiny voice asking if the other man was right. What if Hollis had hallucinated this morning? Or seen a natural trick of the light? Some reflection off the rock face.

No. He was certain of what he'd seen.

"Out of all the men in this company, I didn't think it'd be you who turned against me."

A muscle in Owen's jaw jumped. "I'm not against you—"

"But you think you'd make a better leader."

Owen rolled his shoulders. "August and I have made this journey together. The company needs stability."

And Hollis couldn't give them that, his words implied.

"I'm still the leader of this company," Hollis said. "Whether you like it or not."

Owen wheeled his mount and rode off without another word, leaving Hollis to another quick scan of the terrain. With his thoughts whirling, anger stirred up, he couldn't concentrate.

Whoever was out here had covered his tracks too well. There was no sign of him, even for a seasoned tracker like Hollis. And with his gut churning with betrayal, he couldn't focus enough to see any small sign.

Owen was a strong leader. It was why Hollis counted on him to be one of the captains. Folks listened when Owen talked. But if Owen started talking mutiny, or about splitting off, that might lead to disaster.

He couldn't let that happen.

Twelve

THE FIRE WAS DYING when Hollis came to his bedroll. It was late, there was no noise in camp. No one else awake, save the three men on watch, outside the circle of wagons.

He'd planned it this way. It was easier tiptoeing through the darkness. Better than facing a smiling Abigail over his supper plate, his stomach churning and his heart twisting inside him.

He toed off his boots, aware that she slept a scant arm's reach away, and piled his slicker and hat atop them. A biting wind had blown since late afternoon and brought back a chill he'd thought they had already seen the last of. Most folks in the company bundled up in shawls or blankets as darkness closed in.

Which is why Hollis expected to slip his feet into a cold bedroll. Yet the cloth around his feet was... warm. He ratcheted up on his elbow, but of course it was too dark to see. He toed around and located the large, flat rock still emanating a pleasing heat.

Abigail must've done this. He knew it instantly. She would've placed the large rock in the fire, let it sit there for hours, then tucked it inside his bedroll to warm it.

He lay flat on his back, his head pillowed on one arm. There was too much quiet coming from her bedroll, only those inches away. No even breaths like he'd hear if she was sleeping. She was awake, even though it was late.

Staring up at the countless stars, he felt a heavy weight pressing in on his chest. It'd been a long while since someone had taken care of him. Since someone had thought of his needs, of his comfort.

What did she want from him? He'd told her from the beginning that this marriage couldn't be real.

Her expectations felt crushing on top of the weight he carried about his captains, the company today. He couldn't breathe. He turned onto his shoulder, the movement pushing air out of his lungs in one big *oopmh*.

And now his field of vision locked on Abigail, a shadow in the darkness.

So close. Right there.

"Are you all right?" she whispered, the words barely audible. "I saw Leo and Owen arguing when I was cleaning up from supper; I think you and August were scouting ahead..."

No, he wasn't all right. There'd been tension among the captains in the meeting he'd held during the noonday stop. Cutting glances between the men, silent stares, and crossed arms. An echo of that first fateful overland crossing. He'd been worrying on the problem all day, unsure of how to solve it.

No, he wasn't all right.

Was Owen right? That was the thread that tangled in

Hollis's thoughts. Thoughts of Dinah, Abigail, and his past. Thoughts that stirred him in a way that had never happened to him before. Even before the river had washed him away, if he admitted it to himself.

Was he distracted? Was he putting this company in danger? A liability because of the head injury he'd sustained weeks ago?

"Owen is bucking my leadership." He hadn't meant to blurt out the words, not even in a whisper. But everything that had been eating at him was suddenly unbearable. And she'd asked.

He kicked at the bedroll now stifling his feet, but it didn't help. Because the pressure was coming from inside of him.

A quiet breath. "Owen respects you."

He doubted that, not after how the other man had come after him that morning.

She must've sensed his silent disagreement, even in the dark.

"He found out about the short-term memory problems." August had revealed his secret. Hollis still couldn't come to grips with that.

She made a little sound of understanding, one that grated against his nerves.

"He's hurt you didn't confide in him," she whispered.

"Not hurt. Angry."

"You sure about that?"

He pictured Owen's craggy face from earlier. He was certain.

"You've trusted Owen as one of your captains for the entire journey thus far."

Yes, but he doesn't trust me.

The words caught painfully behind Hollis's chest. The stars that had been bright and warm now sparkled with cold fire. "If Owen doesn't do as I say, it could cause trouble for the company."

He heard a soft sigh. She hesitated before whispering, "You hold to your control so tightly..."

"That's my job," he snapped, voice louder than he intended. A nearby snore was interrupted momentarily before kicking back up. "That's what every one of these families has paid me to do," he whispered fiercely. "To keep them safe and help them reach Oregon."

Owen was too sure of himself. He knew the outdoors and had crossed successfully with his brother, but two men traveling alone could cover different ground, take different risks. A big company was another animal entirely.

"You trusted me and August with your secret," she whispered. "Why not—?"

"Maybe that was a mistake."

Silence settled between them as cold as the air biting the exposed skin of his face. He felt her hurt. Hated that he'd caused it.

But another part of him wondered whether it was for the best. There was no future for him with Abigail. Wasn't it better for her to realize now that there was no fixing his problems? Her compassion was wasted on him.

His voice was rough when he spoke again, "What about you?" he demanded in a whisper. "You don't share what plagues you."

He heard a soft, tearful snort. "Everything plagues me," she returned. "Every day brings different dangers. A new way to lose a friend. Another threat that we may not make it to the Willamette Valley."

"And yet you walk around singing and humming until you drive everyone to distraction."

No, not everyone.

Him.

It was him she drove to distraction.

He'd catch sight of her smile from across camp and feel that tug in his gut. Hear a tinkle of her humming, even if he couldn't see her, and find a smile playing about his lips.

"If there truly is uncertainty around every bend, why shouldn't I greet it with optimism?"

"You can pretend to be happy, but if it isn't real, aren't you lying? To yourself and everyone around you?" The words were out of his mouth before he'd thought them through, before he'd considered their sharpness and how they might strike.

She went silent, barely even breathing. For a moment, he wanted to apologize, to say he hadn't meant them. But before he'd figured out how to get the words out, she rolled away from him in the darkness.

The fire popped. It wasn't loud enough to cover the sound of her soft sniffle. Her shuddering breath.

He'd made her cry.

Knowing he wouldn't sleep, not now, he slipped from his bedroll and left her and the dying fire behind. He didn't know where to go—he needed to stay close in case anyone came looking for him in the night—but he couldn't bear the physical closeness to her, not when things would never work between them.

He'd only taken a step or two outside the circle of wagons when a shadow appeared out of the darkness.

"August."

His friend slipped from his horse and approached. Hollis had forgotten he'd been on watch.

"What's the matter?" August asked.

"Nothing. Everything." Hollis ran his hand through his hair, only now realizing he'd left his hat behind by the fire.

"Abigail?"

"She makes me..."

"Out of sorts?" There was a definite note of amusement in August's voice, one that Hollis couldn't match.

August seemed to read the tension vibrating through him. The man was mindful and observant. It made him a great tracker, but Hollis could've done without it in this moment. He braced for what his friend would say.

"It took Felicity being grabbed by that bandit for me to realize I was the only one standing in the way of my own happiness." August's words were quiet and contemplative. He glanced at Hollis in the darkness. "I've seen you weather a lot of hardship leading this company, but I've never seen you as settled as when we found you and Abigail by the river."

"That wasn't real," Hollis insisted.

August let the words hang in the silent darkness between them. His horse snuffled softly in the grass.

Wasn't it? Hollis could hear the words August would've said.

Or maybe that was his own conscience.

That was part of what was driving him to distraction since they'd returned to the company. The memories of his time with Sparrow were so clear. They'd weathered hours fraught with hardship and tension, yet he had felt settled. Almost happy, if that was possible in the dangerous wilds.

"It wasn't real," he repeated.

"Why can't it be?" August asked gently. "You've got a chance to make it real in these weeks before we reach the end of our journey."

"I can't." That truth settled inside him with a deep finality.

"How come?"

"It isn't my destiny to have that."

"What? A wife? A family? Happiness?"

"Any of it. I figured that out after I lost Dinah. I'm cursed." There was almost a relief to finally saying the words. Acknowledging what he'd been so slow to realize. Dinah had been the last loss in a life full of losses. He couldn't take any more. He'd had his fill of grief.

At least August didn't poke fun. He wasn't that kind of man. "I'm not sure the Bible teaches that a man can be cursed like that. Even Job lost everything... but got it all back."

Hollis shook his head.

"You sure you're meant to suffer like that?" August asked.

If there'd been a hint of skepticism in his friend's tone, Hollis wouldn't have answered. "It's easier to go through life *without*," without happiness, without love, "than to lose it over and over again."

August placed his hand on Hollis's shoulder. "God never promised to keep his people from trouble," he said. "But he did promise He'd never abandon you."

August's words didn't touch him. Hollis felt only hollow.

* * *

You can pretend to be happy.

Hollis's words from last night wouldn't stop ringing in Abigail's ears.

Morning had dawned, but her husband hadn't come to the fire searching for his breakfast. Or anything else. She must have driven him away with her impertinent questions.

What a fool she'd been to think that his openness when he'd spoken of his wife meant that he welcomed her questions and opinions. He'd told her straight from the beginning that this wasn't any kind of real relationship, hadn't he?

She put down the spoon she'd been using to flip a slice of ham browning in the frying pan, only to realize she'd misjudged and the spoon fell to the ground with a thud.

Frowning, she picked it up and set it aside. Another dish to wash.

She hadn't slept well after Hollis left the campfire last night. She'd lain awake for what felt like forever, waiting for him to return. He never had. At some point, she'd drifted off only to dream of murky water pulling her under the surface. Hollis's words ringing in her ears. And then a glimpse of a tall, stately woman—faceless—standing with Hollis before a preacher.

It was that image that had woken her with a gasp. Hollis and his wife, the way Abigail had imagined her.

"Mrs. Fordham said she'd appreciate some more of your broth."

Abigail lifted her head, only then noticing that Felicity had approached.

The camp was bustling around them, everyone preparing for the bugle's call and the orders to roll out.

Mrs. Allen waved to Abigail from her wagon nearby, a reminder that her social standing had improved after the announcement of their marriage. Folks had come to her yesterday to offer their congratulations and to ask how she was faring.

Abigail blinked and pulled herself back into the conversation. Felicity watched her expectantly.

"Of course." She moved to the wagon where she'd left the clean bowls that morning to dry. The broth was on the coals to keep warm. She'd reheated the leftovers of what she'd made last night.

"I don't suppose August would shoot me another grouse? Or turkey? Or quail?" She'd seen Mrs. Ward by the riverbank this morning when she'd gone for water. The woman had been performing the same chore, but looked pale. Abigail could only hope that whatever illness was plaguing their camp wouldn't spread.

Best to be prepared. Mam had taught her that.

"I'll ask." Felicity took the bowl with its fragrant, steaming liquid. "Are you all right?"

"Of course." Abigail smiled at her friend, the words coming naturally. Until Hollis's voice echoed in her mind again. *You can pretend to be happy.*

Felicity's expression turned thoughtful as she glanced toward Ben, who was playing with young Sara, Leo and Evangeline's little girl. Felicity had enough to worry about. Abigail's troubles were her own. Talking about them wouldn't solve anything.

Felicity sidled closer. "I've counted you as a dear friend from the moment we set out on this journey."

Abigail's brows pinched.

"I know that your marriage to Hollis isn't real," Felicity whispered.

A prick of awareness skittered up Abigail's spine. She couldn't help a quick glance around. No one seemed to be paying them any attention.

"Of course it's real." A moment of their vows clicked into the front of her mind.

"I don't see how it could be," Felicity whispered. "One moment you aren't married and then you are?" Her expression grew serious. "Hollis is a hard man."

Abigail frowned. " Only because life has treated him so poorly."

He'd lost his cousin, his wife and baby. If anyone had a reason to keep people at a distance, it was him.

"He has bossed you since the first day of our journey," Felicity reminded her. "Along with everyone else."

"My brother tasked him with watching out for me," Abigail reminded her.

"Yes, but he's—"

"He's a protector," she said with a fierceness she hadn't meant to bleed into her voice. She couldn't bear for her friend to say anything more disparaging about Hollis. "He cares about each soul in this company and keeping each of us safe until the end. He's a warrior who will fight if needed. He's intelligent and articulate—"

"All right," Felicity said, holding one hand in front of her.

Abigail was breathing hard, like she'd run circles around her wagon. She hadn't meant to get so riled up.

"I can see that your feelings toward him have grown since we started this journey."

Felicity's statement hit with a gravity Abigail hadn't expected. She leaned one hip against the tailgate, her hand landing on its surface to steady her. Until this moment she hadn't realized how deeply her feelings about Hollis ran. What had begun as a grudging friendship had grown into something more—for her.

Yet with the same weight, she realized the futility of caring for him.

"Then you've made a good match," Felicity said. "Even though you forgot to invite your closest friend to the ceremony."

Ah. There was the hurt that had kept Felicity at a distance yesterday and brought on her chilly words moments ago.

"I'm sorry," Abigail said. "It happened so quickly—"

"And I've been distracted with August and Ben. Then you were swept away, and we were frantic to find you." Felicity seemed as eager to believe the timing as Hollis and Owen had hoped everyone in the company would be.

Abigail hated keeping the truth from her friend; her stomach knotted and she opened her mouth to say the whole truth. That Hollis wasn't a good match for her because he didn't want a wife. That the marriage would be dissolved in Oregon. That Abigail's heart would be broken.

But she snapped her mouth closed and swallowed it all.

"I'm thankful for your friendship," she said before sharing a quick hug with her friend.

Felicity held up the bowl. "I'd better deliver this broth before it chills."

She disappeared, but it wasn't long before a young man ran up calling for Hollis.

"He's not here," Abigail said. "I believe he's with his captains."

It was her best guess, given that her husband hadn't graced her with his presence this morning.

"Our neighbor is awful sick this morning," he said. "I'm gonna help them get their oxen in the traces, but the husband looks like he's gonna fall over iffen he has to walk far this morning. Can you tell him?"

"Of course."

She pushed down everything that had been worrying her about her relationship with Hollis to deal with at a later time. It didn't matter whether Hollis wanted to see her. This news was something he needed to hear. It might even affect the entire company.

She left her packing to search for him but found him nowhere among the wagons. She strained her eyes to see the cowboys guarding Leo and Evangeline's herd of cattle.

Not there either.

It was a relief to see Owen riding through the chaos of families packing up. After last night, she knew that there was tension between the two men. But she also believed what she'd said about Owen. He'd earned Hollis's trust over the past weeks on the trail.

He was clearly impatient to be away when she waved him down.

"Can you get a message to Hollis?" she asked. "The Kimball family is very ill this morning. They may need help driving the wagon."

"I'll make sure they get the help they need."

She felt a moment of misgiving. "And tell Hollis," she repeated.

He nodded, wheeling his horse. Or had that been a shake of his head? He was already gone, so she couldn't press him more. Owen was busy. It was a lot of work to get the company moving from the circle. But he'd get word to Hollis.

Thirteen

"I DROPPED MY SPOON!"

"I need more biscuit."

Abigail rested a hand on baby Ambrose's tummy. She'd laid him on a blanket after she'd finally figured out that his constant crying wasn't over the tooth his four-year-old brother Ishmael thought he was cutting but the soaking wet diaper he wore. Now he smiled at her with one brown fist in his mouth, dark eyes dancing as he gurgled.

It'd been a long day of travel. Folks were plumb worn out. These children's parents had fallen ill, so Abigail had offered to help while the parents got some rest.

"Stay there," she told the brown-skinned Ishmael and his toddler sister Charity. The two young children sat on a crate and short barrel, respectively. She watched them for a moment to ensure they were doing what she'd said, and then went back to diapering the youngest.

Abigail hadn't realized what a miserable state the Fordhams were in. The family was quiet, never caused trouble, kept to themselves. No one in the company had noticed that their food supplies were dwindling. They needed to purchase more flour, salt, and other staples at the fort, or they would run out of supplies before they reached the mountain passes.

Keziah Fordham had been suffering from stomach pains and couldn't keep any food down; her husband was worse off. After Abigail had been called to help them, she'd spent the first part of the evening preparing a quick supper for the children, who were badly in need of baths and their clothes a wash. Abigail had been run off her feet trying to keep up with them after the wagons had circled this evening.

She hefted the baby into her arms and moved to where she'd left the biscuit pan near the fire to keep bugs away.

"I'm full," four-year-old Ishmael said when she offered him the biscuit.

The baby gripped the shoulder of her dress in one soggy fist.

"I done!" Charity, the toddler, spoke non-stop, but many of her words were gibberish to Abigail's ears.

"She's done," Ishmael echoed.

"Let's clean up—" before Abigail could get the words out, both children had tipped their plates onto the ground, splattering what was left of their food on the ground. They jumped up and began tussling.

"Stop! You're too close to the fire!" She moved to grab one of them, her skirt swishing too near to the flames for comfort.

"What's going on here?" Hollis's voice boomed, startling her and earning a cry from the baby.

Hollis stepped between the two children and the fire, scooping Ishmael into a hold he might've used for a sack of flour, the boy pressed horizontally next to his side.

Abigail swayed gently side to side, patting the baby's back. Hollis's questioning eyes met hers.

"I came looking for you. Evangeline said you'd been over here all evening." His gaze was almost... concerned?

No doubt he'd finally gotten hungry enough to seek out his supper—he'd skipped both breakfast and lunch—only to find the fire cold and no food to be found. She felt a vague sense of satisfaction that then caused a brief flare of guilt.

"These hooligans needed someone to feed them their supper," she said.

She'd sent word to him earlier about the Kimball family; the Fordhams were their nearest neighbors in the wagon train. He'd have heard that they were ill, too.

He raised his brows as he looked at the mess left by the two plates, now seeping into the ground. Looked at her attempting to calm the baby.

No doubt she was disheveled and probably covered with remnants of food—the baby had been challenging to feed, constantly pushing away the spoon. When she'd given in to him to attempt to feed himself, he'd flung little bits of mashed potatoes at her.

But Hollis's eyes were warm.

"Children," he said with a pointed look at the two little ones staring wide-eyed at him, "it's time we helped Mrs. Abigail clean up."

Mrs. Abigail.

The honorific in front of her name did something

twisty to her insides, and she turned away. Humming to the baby came naturally. She'd never had nieces or nephews, not even little cousins to snuggle.

Behind her, Hollis instructed Ishmael and Charity to clean up. Ambrose finally calmed, lying his head on her shoulder. Or perhaps he'd just worn himself out. He'd been inconsolable all evening. Missing his mam?

The sun was quickly heading toward the horizon. Her own stomach growled. Between feeding all three of the little ones, Abigail hadn't had a bite to eat herself.

Still humming, she turned to find that Hollis and the children had made quick work of cleaning up the mess. Hollis had found the bucket of clean water she'd stashed beneath the wagon, halfway behind one of the wagon wheels. Out of the way of small feet that would knock it over. Both Ishmael and Charity's faces and hands were clean. That was surely good enough for tonight.

Hollis must've seen the admiration in her look, but his eyes cut away.

"There's a pallet already laid inside the wagon," she murmured to Hollis. To the little ones, she put a cheery note in her voice. "It's time for bed. Why don't you climb into the wagon?"

Hollis bent to help Ishmael with his boots while she kept the baby on her shoulder as she squatted to help Charity with her shoes.

"Tanks fer supp'r," she said with a sweet, shy smile.

Before she could brace herself, Charity threw her arms around Abigail's neck. She wobbled, the unexpected movement throwing her off balance.

Hollis steadied her with one hand between her shoulders.

"You're welcome," she breathed through the tight hug around her neck, unexpected tears pricking her eyes.

What would it be like to have a child of her own, a family of her own? She hadn't thought about it for a very long time. After Mr. Smith had betrayed her, she'd been so focused on reaching Oregon, on finding her brother and settling, that she had put such thoughts out of her mind completely.

But as the girl moved away and Hollis helped Abigail straighten with a hand beneath her elbow, her shoulder brushed his broad chest. Felicity's words from the morning burst into the forefront of her mind. *A good match.*

Hollis gazed down into her face and, for a moment, his glance appeared to encompass the babe on her shoulder. A soft light filled his eyes, the shadow of pain shifting into something else—something that looked like wanting.

Her breath caught, lodging behind her sternum.

And then the moment broke.

Hollis moved away, helping Ishmael crawl up into the wagon in his sock feet. Abigail peered over the wagon's side as Hollis, with his greater height, reached in and pulled a quilt over the two children. They looked terrified, their eyes wide in their faces.

"What if wolves come 'n get us?" Ishmael whispered.

"Wolves," Charity echoed.

Abigail's heart squeezed. "Your mam and papa are sleeping in the tent, right there," she said, pointing over their heads to the tent just behind the wagon, where it was quieter.

"There are lots of men watching over the camp," Hollis said solemnly.

"Watchin' for wolves?"

The big, tough man nodded with a gentle seriousness. "You'll be safe."

Ishmael turned his gaze on Abigail. "I like that song you was hummin'. Wouldja sing it?"

"Pwease?" Charity had the biggest set of pleading eyes Abigail'd ever seen.

She began to sing the lullaby she'd learned from her mother. On her shoulder, Ambrose went relaxed and limp.

"You sing," Charity demanded of Hollis.

Abigail kept singing, waiting for the wagon master to refuse. Only to feel a bolt of shock when he joined her, his bass an octave deeper than her alto. She couldn't seem to look away from him, though he kept his eyes on the children in the wagon.

Hollis was singing.

He stumbled over the words at first. His voice was rough—from disuse? A note missed here and there. She couldn't stop wondering how long it had been since he'd sung—this song or any song.

He'd been so lost to his grief. And now—

Hope trilled through her on the wings of this lullaby.

She stood near enough to slip her hand, the one not holding the babe, into his larger one. She couldn't look at him when she'd done it, not when she expected him to drop her hand as if burned. To reject her.

But he didn't.

He held on.

And turned toward her, the motion turning her, too, so that they stood face to face as the last notes of the lullaby faded away.

* * *

What kind of spell was Abigail weaving over him?

Hollis went quiet, his throat raw from singing—or maybe from the memories that had flowed through him, the grief that had at once pricked him, and now flowed away like water running down a hill.

It wasn't gone, not completely. But healing, leaving a scar.

He was peripherally aware of the two Fordham kids with their heads together, whispering, just out of sight inside that wagon, and the soft sigh from the baby drifting to sleep on Abigail's shoulder.

In sharp relief was the beat of heat, like a jagged lightning strike, running from their linked fingers and pressed together palms.

He was mesmerized by the brown pools of her eyes. She was... happy with him. A quiet joy flowing from her into his heart. He couldn't help leaning closer. Close enough to feel the sweet warmth of her breath on his chin, count the individual eyelashes surrounding each eye.

He distinctly remembered the feel of her lips pressed to his. He could taste—

"Don't kiss me if you don't mean it." The vulnerable whisper drew him back to his senses.

He let go of her, took a step back. He reached up to remove his hat, push a hand through his hair.

What had he been thinking?

He hadn't been, that much was clear.

But his heart was still throbbing in his throat, and he wanted to pull her into his arms.

She watched him with soft eyes. Her hand came up to rub the sleeping baby's back. "I care about you," she said with a quiet seriousness that hit low in his belly.

He wanted to deny the words, the connection they implied. He couldn't—

"I think you care about me, too."

Something hot sliced through his insides. His nostrils flared. "I'm attracted to you."

He could admit that. Surely she already knew.

"I think it's more than that," she challenged with a lift of her chin, something deeper in her eyes. "It's been between us since the beginning of this journey. Since before either one of us was willing to admit to it."

He shook his head slowly but still couldn't tear his eyes from her. If she touched him, it might set off the tension vibrating through his entire self. He felt like a keg of powder. Ready to explode.

He was poised to run.

She didn't move toward him.

"I don't want an annulment. I want our marriage to be real." Her lips firmed into a line, her chin lifted with determination. But he saw the uncertainty in her eyes even as his chest ballooned with panic.

The baby made a soft noise and nuzzled his face into her collarbone.

Something that had been niggling in the back of Hollis's mind solidified. He grasped onto it, grateful for something else to focus on. "You said their parents are asleep. Why?"

She glanced at the tent just beyond the wagon. "They're sick. The Kimballs, too." Her brow creased with concern. "I sent Owen with a message for you earlier."

Frustration fired. "Why didn't you tell me yourself?"

"Because you've been avoiding me," she returned with a

bite to the words. "Owen was nearby and I knew—I thought he'd give you the message."

"He didn't." Anger stirred. He tamped it down to deal with Owen later. "How bad off are they?"

His spirits sank as she listed off the same symptoms four other families had experienced. He couldn't deny it any more. They were facing the beginning of an epidemic.

"I need to think," he told her as his stomach growled, reminding him he hadn't eaten. There wasn't time for that now.

She moved toward the Fordhams' tent as he stalked off.

He reached for his pocket, for the leather bound book that he needed to help him parse an answer. But the book wasn't there. He had left it on the wagon wheel when he'd arrived in camp and found Abigail absent.

As he strode into the small section of camp Abigail had carved out for the two of them, Owen approached from the opposite direction, Leo on his heels.

Hollis gritted his teeth as he reached for the logbook. He didn't even want to look at Owen right now. If there was any sign that this man was undermining Hollis's leadership, it was that he hadn't delivered Abigail's message. If he'd been too busy to do it himself, he could've sent someone.

"We've got another two families sick," Leo was the one who spoke.

"Four more," a soft, feminine voice said from the shadows. Maddie, drying her hands, approaching from outside the camp. She must've been washing up at the creek.

Hollis felt the news like a physical blow.

"All the same symptoms?" he asked. There was no time

for personal feelings in this moment. He had to put his frustration with Owen aside in favor of helping the company as best he could.

"Doc thinks its—"

"Typhoid." Owen and Maddie spoke at the same time. Maddie scowled a bit—why? He didn't have time to figure that out, either.

He flipped to the small leaf he'd used as a bookmark earlier today. Read quickly from the page. "We're only two days from the fort," he said.

Owen was already shaking his head. "Doc says if we push too hard, folks won't get the rest they need. They'll die."

Fire licked inside of Hollis. "If we get caught on the mountains too late, we'll all die," he reminded his captain in a tight voice.

"There'll be folks to help at the fort," Maddie interjected.

Abigail had joined them, Hollis realized belatedly. She hung back near the wagon, a few steps from Maddie.

Trust Owen.

Abigail's words from last night blasted through his memory, but he rejected them. Owen didn't deserve his trust. Not now.

"This company is still under my leadership—"

"What kind of leadership doesn't care whether you lose families to sickness?" Owen demanded.

"Hang on," Leo said, with a hand out to try and calm his half-brother.

"I do care," Hollis ground out. Ten lost. The number from his logbook was always on his mind. He didn't want to add to it. "That's why reaching the fort is imperative."

"Doc says—"

"Doc isn't the leader of this company," Hollis burst out. "And neither are you. I won't let you stay on with my company if you keep challenging my decisions."

The words hung between them. Owen stared and Hollis held his gaze, determined not to be the first to look away.

Leo said something to Owen that Hollis couldn't hear. Hopefully asking him to see reason.

Owen scowled. He whipped his hat off and dusted it against his pant leg.

Hollis turned to Maddie, who was watching with wide, serious eyes. "You've been our camp nurse all these weeks. Can folks make it to the fort?"

She hesitated. It was small, but it was there. "I think so. They might have some medicine that will help. Food stores that some of the families need."

He'd learned to trust his instincts, and they were telling him that the right thing was to move. He caught Abigail's eye momentarily, quickly looking away.

I want our marriage to be real.

If she was close enough, if they were in private, she'd ask him whether he was pushing on out of stubbornness. Somehow he knew it.

He wasn't. But the uncertainty gnawed at his gut.

Owen stomped off, and Maddie said something low to Abigail before scurrying off into the center of camp.

Leo walked around the campfire to come face to face with Hollis. "If Owen leaves the company, August will, too."

Was it a warning, or a threat? Leo considered Hollis seriously and Hollis had to wonder if Owen had told him about the memory problems. Were all of Hollis's captains questioning his authority?

"And what about you?" Hollis demanded. "Will you leave?"

The larger wagon train offered more protection for Leo and his brothers' herd of cattle, offered a watch at night to help out the cowboys that Leo had hired earlier in the journey.

A smaller wagon train would make an easier target. Leo had to know that.

When Leo rubbed one hand down his face, Hollis noticed how peaked he looked. Was he sick, too?

"I don't know," Leo said. "I need to talk to Alice. Evangeline. And my brothers." Leo had more to protect than when he'd left Independence. His wife had a wagon full of gold hidden among her things. Leo had a daughter now. Surely he'd see Owen's stubbornness for the bad idea it was.

Hollis let him go, frustration and concern boiling into an inferno inside him.

Then Abigail was there, offering him a biscuit with a piece of ham squished into the middle. "Eat."

He hated that she saw what was gnawing at him inside. Her words from earlier wouldn't leave him alone, like buzzing bees.

Distracted.

He couldn't afford to be distracted. Not with an epidemic on his hands.

"I have nothing to give you," he said. "That's my answer."

He saw the stricken expression on her face but forced himself to turn away.

It was too painful to hope and then have everything good ripped away from him. He needed focus now more than ever.

Marrying her had been a mistake. One he never should've made.

Fourteen

TWO DAYS LATER, Abigail dipped a small cloth into a pail of cool water and even the effort to lift it back out felt like climbing a mountain. All she wanted to do was lie down.

This wasn't the time for that. She knew it. And yet...

She forced the notes of mama's lullaby from her chest in a hum as she dragged her arm up, wrung out the cloth, and then used it to dab the brow of a young boy lying on a pallet on the ground next to his parents' wagon, burning up with fever. His parents fared no better, sleeping next to him, faces pink with fever.

After Abigail had done what she could to cool the boy's face and neck, then dribbled a scant few drops of water in his mouth, she stood on shaky legs, wiping her brow with the back of her hand. She took the pail with her. Where was she needed now?

Afternoon sunlight warmed her, pricking her skin with tiny beads of sweat. The fort stood several hundred yards away, a grouping of squat buildings behind a barricade that appeared half-built. Or maybe someone had started it and given up. Hollis was there, bringing help.

That was her only solace as the weight of the pail pulled her shoulders down. They had pushed the oxen faster and longer so that they could reach the fort as soon as possible. But almost half the company had been left behind. Abigail missed Felicity dearly, and it'd only been thirty-six hours since she'd seen her friend.

She traded out the pail of used water for a clean, fresh one with a dipper inside. She leaned against the nearest wagon, taking respite in the shade of its canopy. Just for a moment.

Surely Hollis would arrive with help soon.

Hollis had been taciturn and pensive, almost angry, since the company had split. She didn't know how to help him, how to let him know that he wasn't alone. He didn't want her for a wife, but at one time she'd been his friend. Maybe she could still be that.

She slipped her hand into her pocket and felt the edges of a piece of folded paper inside. She brought it out, needing the comfort from her brother's letter. She'd found it tucked in one of the books Evangeline had lent her, still in Abigail's wagon. The letter was one of the only things of Abigail's that hadn't been destroyed or lost when the twister had decimated the wagon she and Felicity had shared at that time.

She unfolded it and ran her fingers over the artful script. Her brother had always had an affinity for learning. She could remember him sitting at the table in mama's work kitchen, practicing his letters.

Longing gripped her. When would she see her beloved

brother? Surely his presence would provide the stability she had been aching for since her boss's betrayal.

Hollis strode across the expanse between the fort and wagons. Alone.

The set of the wagonmaster's shoulders radiated tension. Abigail's stomach knotted as she waited for his approach.

He took the dipper from her and paused in the wagon's shadow, expression grim.

"No one is coming to help," she guessed.

His eyes were shuttered. He handed back the dipper. "They won't let any of us come in the fort, not with typhoid among our group." He looked so defeated. "And they won't send their doctor—or anyone else—to help."

She felt breathless fear, worry that must be an echo of his own. *What will we do?*

He glanced down at her hand, where she still clutched the letter. "What's that?"

Did he need a distraction? She could provide that. "Joseph's last letter to me." She pressed it against her chest, wishing it was her brother himself. "I don't know how he managed to send money for my passage. God's providence, I suppose. Joseph didn't know about Mr. Smith."

Hollis's brows drew together. "What about Mr. Smith?"

The old betrayal sliced through her. "Mr. Smith promised to help me save for the trip since I couldn't open a bank account. He stole my money."

She felt Hollis's stillness beside her. Pushed on to finish the story. "He didn't want me to leave. Didn't want to have to find another cook for the family, I suppose." The feeling that he'd wanted to trap her still made her insides clench tight.

"It wasn't right," Hollis said, his nostrils flaring. "Did you tell the authorities?"

"No. I just... left. And found Joseph's gift waiting for me."

Hollis's eyes watched the horizon now. "Joseph saved me once too. On that first journey I took across the prairie."

He blinked, stirred. As if he hadn't meant to say that. "I saw him the last time my train reached the Willamette Valley. He was hale, and..." His eyes shadowed briefly. "He couldn't keep his eyes off a young woman from a neighboring village."

Joseph? He'd always been more interested in his books than in young women.

Hollis shifted his feet. "I wouldn't be surprised if you arrive to find them married."

Unease slithered through Abigail. Hollis glanced behind her, as if to check on the camp, unaware of the turmoil his words had caused.

Joseph had sent for Abigail, had painted a grand picture of the new business he'd help her get started out in Oregon. A cafe, where she could put her skills in the kitchen toward crafting her own future.

She wanted it. A business that was hers to run. The stability of building a clientele of repeat customers, always knowing she'd have an income. No Mr. Smith to steal from her. She would be her own boss.

But if Joseph had a new wife, what if that woman didn't want him to spend their money helping Abigail get her business off the ground?

Maddie ducked out of the Carters' wagon and caught sight of them as she climbed down the wagon wheel. She headed their way. Hollis moved to intercept her, speaking urgently.

Abigail should go and check on the next family. The Wards? Or someone else? It was difficult to order her thoughts. The sun was on its descent. Did it feel hotter out here?

She was pushing off the wagon when Maddie reached her.

"I was just going to check on Mrs. Madigan," Abigail said.

A sadness showed in Maddie's expression. "She's gone."

For a moment, Abigail felt nothing. And then a rush of grief. Mrs. Madigan had been a lovely older woman who had been like a grandmother to many folks on the wagon train. She'd always had a kind word to say.

Gone.

Abigail's eyes skipped past Maddie to Hollis, who was kneeling next to Mr. Fordham, who'd risen up on one elbow.

"Does he know?" Abigail whispered.

"I just told him."

Hollis's mouth was grim as he spoke to Mr. Fordham. He would have another loss to write in his logbook. He'd gotten the awful news, and he'd gone right to work. He hadn't said one word of comfort to her.

I have nothing to give you.

He'd said the words two days ago. She'd known what they'd meant, but somewhere deep inside, she'd held onto a thread of hope. One so thin and frayed that it snapped now, and she felt herself sink into a mire of emptiness.

Hollis had told her, repeatedly, that he didn't want a second wife. He didn't want her.

Abigail was the one who had chosen to hope, to believe that she might be enough to change his mind.

There was loss all around her. So much loss.

And what was waiting for her in Oregon? More uncertainty. Perhaps things had changed too much between her and her brother since he'd left four years ago.

Would she never find the peace she craved?

"Abigail?"

She heard Maddie's voice as if from far away, but suddenly, everything was too much. Too much grief, too much pain.

Too hot.

"I need to sit down." She said the words. Or tried to. The pail slipped from suddenly nerveless fingers as her legs grew weak.

"Abigail!"

She felt Maddie's arm—strong for such a slight woman —grab her waist, felt the scratch of grass as she was lowered to the ground.

"Hollis!"

Abigail had lost her sight—no, her eyes had simply closed. She forced them open, saw a hand, felt a cool touch on her forehead. She focused on the sky, with high, wispy clouds skittering to the south.

"She's burning up."

Her eyes had slid closed again. Was that Maddie speaking?

"Open your eyes." *Definitely* Hollis's voice, the command deep and gravelly. She didn't dare disobey.

Tears slipped from her eyes as she opened them to meet

his intent stare. His cool hand rested on the skin of her jaw and cheek.

"My head hurts," she whispered.

Was she the only one burning up?

"I'm sorry." Sorry she couldn't be enough for him to love. Sorry for everything he'd lost. Sorry for the little boy who'd grieved so fiercely.

"Don't drift off," he ordered. "Stay awake."

But this time, she couldn't make her body listen.

She slipped into darkness.

Hollis felt the bottom of his stomach drop out as Abigail's fever-bright eyes closed.

"Abigail. Abby. Wake up."

She didn't respond. He still held his palm against her cheek and tapped her with his forefinger.

Maddie let go of Abigail's wrist, where she'd been counting the beats of her heart.

"How long has she had the fever?" Maddie asked.

He shook his head, helplessness rolling over him like a rogue wave in an overflowing river. Despair threatened to suck him under. "I don't know." He could barely get the words out, and when he did, they were rough with emotion.

He had been too scared to get close to her in these past days since they'd left the wagon train. Scared of himself— of what he'd do if he got near enough to clasp her hand in his again.

Two days ago, he'd almost kissed her. Had barely come to his senses in time. Or maybe didn't have any sense left, not when his instincts kept urging him to turn to her, to grab onto her and not let go.

"Please, not her." He didn't know where the guttural whisper came from. He bowed his head, fighting the tears that wouldn't help anything. He was still reeling from the news that Mrs. Madigan had passed. He knew—he knew!—how this sickness could kill.

And now Abigail...

He couldn't even think about what losing her might mean to him.

"Can you lift her into the wagon?" Maddie pressed.

He raised his head to meet her concerned gaze.

"She'll be more comfortable there," Maddie said.

He had to pull himself together. But he was shaking as he rose to his knees, gathered Abigail to him and stood to his feet.

He could feel her fever heat radiating through her dress and his shirt. He'd thought she looked peaked when he'd spoken to her only moments ago. Why hadn't he asked if she needed to rest?

Because he was a fool.

Maddie looked pale too. Exhausted. In camp, there had been only a handful of folks who hadn't been touched by the typhoid. And Maddie was running herself ragged.

"Is the fort's doctor coming?" Maddie asked as Hollis moved to lay Abigail inside the wagon, where a blanket had already been spread and the crates and barrels shoved to one side.

"No one is coming," he grated out.

He'd felt the helplessness of it, the biting words from a sergeant who had kept a good ten feet from Hollis once he'd understood the company was ill.

"A doctor has a duty to help—" she started.

"Then maybe we should've forced our camp doctor to come with us."

She flinched, and he realized he'd growled the words. Almost bitten her head off.

This wasn't her fault.

"Then... we're on our own?" Her words trembled.

Hollis nodded gravely. "They won't send anyone or allow us into the fort until we're completely well."

Desperation seized him. He'd made the best choice he could, seeking help at the fort. Only to find that he'd perhaps doomed them all.

Owen was right. Hollis wasn't fit to lead this company.

Abigail's head lolled to the side, limp and unresponsive.

"If she can get through the fever..." Maddie trailed off.

He knew. If she fought through the fever, she'd be weak and weary but alive. And if she didn't?

Memories flitted through his mind, too fast for him to catch any of them completely.

Holding Abigail the night they'd been stranded in the woods.

The determined moue she'd made when he'd been barely conscious after his concussion and she'd ordered him to eat.

The turn of her face, a glimpse just long enough to see her dawning smile. Feel the tug in his gut.

Their kiss.

Watching her walk alongside Felicity, in the early days of their journey. Keeping his distance, because if he spoke to her, he'd want to know her.

It's been there between us, from the beginning.

She'd been right. There'd been a recognition inside of

him from the moment he'd seen her on the boardwalk in Independence. A connection that once ignited, he hadn't been able to ignore but fully able to deny.

Looking at her pale skin, her slack expression, he couldn't pretend any longer.

He hadn't meant to, he'd tried his hardest not to, but somehow he'd fallen for her anyway.

And now she was sick. She could die. Just like Dinah. The baby. Charles.

He was going to lose her.

Maddie said something to him, but he couldn't make out the words as he backed out of the wagon and whirled away. He had to get away, escape.

He ran out into the open prairie, ran until his legs burned and his lungs were on fire.

Stopped to lean both hands on his knees. Retched into the prairie grass.

He was cursed. He'd known it for years.

And now he'd cursed Abigail because he'd been too weak to push her away. She'd gotten close, and now he was going to lose her.

He screamed at the sky, a wordless shout that barely touched the pain rolling over him.

Why did God hate him? Why was He punishing Abigail for Hollis's sins, whatever those were?

There was no answer. No strike of lightning to take Hollis's own worthless life.

That would be too easy.

He turned back the way he'd come, wishing for the emptiness he'd known when the berries had stolen his memory. The fort was there, so close but out of reach. The wagons a reminder of all the travelers he'd failed.

He couldn't leave Maddie to tend to the ill by herself. It wasn't fair to do that to her.

Hollis trudged back toward the wagons. What had become of the travelers they'd left behind?

Was the doctor right? Had their isolated patients and extra rest done more than Hollis's pushing to reach the fort? Or was Owen suffering just as he was?

Hollis had no answers. No prayers, no hope of Divine providence. Only a desperate grief that swamped him as he made his way back into the camp.

<h1 style="text-align:center;font-style:italic">Fifteen</h1>

THERE WAS a low groan as Alice passed from the shadows outside the camp to the space near the campfire, now burning low. It was late and she longed for her bedroll, but there was more to be done.

She paused for a moment at the fire to feed it a handful of sticks. It popped and crackled, illuminating the dwindling pile of wood to burn.

Today she'd left camp between bouts of tending her sick family and spent two hours scouring the area for more wood or buffalo chips to burn. Both were growing scarce. They'd stayed too long in one place. And there hadn't been a hunting party to go out since they'd separated from Hollis's company.

Food was growing scarce, too.

The twist in Alice's gut grew stronger and stronger each time she'd passed through the camp checking on other families that seemed to grow sicker and sicker. Women who should've been resting instead cooked over campfires, and Alice recognized the haunted, hungry looks in their eyes.

"Alice, that you?" The faint whisper cut through the darkness. Coop, awake in his bedroll.

Alice left the fire, bringing the pail of water and dipper with her. The moon was out, beautiful and full. Between it and the fire, she saw too clearly the feverish light in his eyes.

She laid a hand on his forehead as her other hand held the dipper steady. He touched the handle, brought it to his lips and guzzled down several sips of water.

He was burning up with fever. He felt even hotter than Leo had when she'd checked on him a half hour ago.

His lips smacked as he finished drinking. He laid his head back down as if the effort of holding it up was too much for him to bear. Groaning slightly, he wrapped one arm around his middle.

"You're an angel, sister," he whispered.

She wasn't. She was a very frightened woman. Coop had held out the longest. For days, he'd helped her tote water, wash soiled laundry, even cook as the entire company took sick. Until this afternoon, when he'd succumbed to the fever and stomach cramps.

"Doc got any more medicine?" Coop asked. His eyes were closed. Would he even remember the conversation, or would it be like a fevered dream the next time he woke?

"The quinine is gone." The doc had told her so himself when the two of them, along with the couple of others who hadn't fallen sick, had gathered for a meeting earlier this afternoon. That seemed so long ago now.

"For all the good it did," she muttered to herself. The medicine hadn't seemed to make a difference. But what did she know? She wasn't a doctor. Maybe it did something on the inside, something she couldn't understand.

Or maybe all of this was futile.

The doctor had grown more and more grim as the days had worn on. Had they traveled all this way only to die out here on this plain?

She'd kept the thought at bay as Leo had gotten sick. Then little Sara, Owen, August, Evangeline, Felicity. Collin and Stella. Coop.

One by one, everyone she loved had yielded to the fever. And not a one of them was improving.

They needed more medicine. Different medicine. Food.

Help. They needed help.

They should've gone along with Hollis to the fort. She wanted to cry thinking about it.

Coop shifted in his bedroll when she straightened. She bent to brush her fingertips across his forehead. "Go back to sleep. You need rest."

He never opened his eyes, just mumbled something she couldn't understand.

Heart pounding, she tiptoed through the tents to the one Leo and Evangeline shared. Leo would know what to do.

But when she pulled back the corner of the canvas flap and shook his shoulder, he didn't wake. A touch to the back of his hand revealed he was still burning up with fever.

Fear choking her, she had only one thought.

Get help.

She left the water pail behind and strode through the darkness to where Leo and her other brothers had left the horses picketed for grazing. A soft whicker met her ears.

Leo's saddle was heavy enough to make her arms shake as she hefted it and brought it to his horse.

The animal stood patiently as she lifted and pushed the saddle onto its back. She was no horsewoman. It took far too long to locate the buckle beneath the horse's stomach. A new frisson of fear skittered down her spine as she imagined the saddle slipping off completely, her with it.

She leaned her forehead into the patient horse's shoulder. What if she couldn't do this?

A footstep crunched in the dry grasses nearby. "That saddle's nearly bigger than you are."

She whirled before she recognized the voice, scrabbling for some weapon to defend herself. When she realized it was Braddock there in the moonlight, her panic receded.

"What are you doing?" The strong moonlight illuminated his drawn face. She'd passed by his wagon once, seen him sickly, working with one hand pressed against his stomach. He hadn't been immune to the epidemic, but who had been looking after him? He was alone within the larger company.

"I'm riding for help." It was silly to answer him. Surely he could see what she was doing. She fumbled with the buckle again.

"Not alone. Where are your brothers?"

When she kept her shoulder turned to him and didn't answer, he pushed again. "You can't mean to go alone."

She knew the danger. Not long ago, wolves had nearly set on August when he'd been out hunting by himself.

But, "I can't sit helplessly in camp and watch my family die."

The crunch of his footsteps faded away. When she turned her head, he was gone.

Awareness tingled in the lobes of her ears. She fumbled with the buckle, finally slipping the leather through the metal clasp. But the saddle still seemed too loose.

Braddock didn't have to like it that she was going. Surely, he knew she must. That attempting to argue with her wouldn't change things.

But what if he'd gone back into camp to fetch one of her brothers? She strained her ears for the sound of arguing, remembering Braddock's bruises from days ago when he'd fought with Coop.

Tears smarted in her eyes when the leather and buckle slipped through her fingers. The horse sidestepped with a soft neigh.

Frustration surged. Worry made her almost frantic. She stepped toward the horse again. The sound of approaching hoofbeats, quiet and slow and thudding into the soft ground, made her heart race.

She grabbed the horse's reins and turned to look.

Braddock again, bareheaded. Leading a horse.

He came straight to her, dropping his horse's reins to the ground when he was a few feet away. He moved to the saddle she'd had trouble with after murmuring something low and incomprehensible to the horse, who had no compunction about allowing Braddock to tend to his saddle.

"What do you think you're doing?" she demanded in a whisper.

"Going with you." He said the words so easily, in such a matter-of-fact manner.

Not like how she blurted, "You can't. It isn't appropriate for us to be alone together."

A flush fired in her cheeks.

He finished with the saddle, giving it a tug to ensure it was secure, and then turned to face her in the moonlight.

"Who's going to stop me? No one else in camp has the strength to sit a horse."

"Neither do you." The familiar feeling of battling words with him stole over her so quickly that it stole her breath. It was easy, so easy, to slip back into the verbal sparring that had begun their secret relationship. The first time she'd snapped at him, she'd frozen in place, certain she was going to be fired from her job as maid in his grandfather's household.

She hadn't been fired.

And their arguments had slowly changed into flirtations.

The reminder of all of it stole her breath and made her words sharp. "I don't want you to go. I don't need you."

The moonlight shone bright enough for her to see the change in his demeanor. Something slipped over his expression, as if he withdrew into himself. He was grave when he said, "Whatever you think about me now, it was never my wish to hurt you."

When should we tell your brothers? She could hear his voice in her memory, so clearly. They had sat on the bank of the creek that snaked through his grandfather's estate, fingers interlaced. *When should we tell your grandfather?* she'd countered.

"I couldn't live with myself if something happened to you," he said quietly.

She couldn't meet his gaze.

She'd spent every day of this journey nursing her hurt. She'd ignored him, ignored any consideration that he might've been hurt too.

It didn't matter, she told herself. He had abandoned her when it had counted most. There was no salvaging anything they'd once had—all of it was lost. The only thing that mattered now was finding help for her family and the others in camp. Nothing else.

"Let's go." She said the words stiffly, moved past him to boost herself into the saddle.

She couldn't help the awareness that he mounted up and pushed his horse into a walk just behind her. She'd ask her horse for a faster pace when they weren't so close to camp.

All of this would be easier if she could simply ignore Braddock. But she'd never been able to do that. Not from the very beginning.

* * *

"Should we send out two men as a hunting party?"

It took a moment for the words to register for Hollis, who'd been staring at the western horizon as the sun rose behind him.

The sky was lighting up, but he felt filled with darkness.

He shook himself and turned his unshaven cheek to Mr. Keller, who stood a little behind him, waiting expectantly. The man was pale and drawn, but at least he stood upright today.

Some of the travelers had begun to overcome the illness and recover.

But not Abigail.

"We've little fresh meat in camp," Mr. Keller said,

pushing for an answer that Hollis didn't feel equipped to give.

"If you need the meat, and there are at least two of you fit to go, then go." His voice emerged coarse, like he hadn't spoken in a week, and Hollis saw the flash of surprise cross the other man's face before he nodded and walked away.

Hollis had spent most of the night with his head in his hands. He couldn't bear to sit at Abigail's side. He'd left that to Maddie, who'd dabbed her forehead with damp cloths to keep the fever down, dribbled water into Abigail's slack mouth.

Hollis had sat outside the camp and mourned. At the center of himself, there was an inferno of anger—and guilt.

He knew better.

He never should've let Abigail close.

Another footstep in the grass and he sighed. He didn't feel capable of leading the wagon train in this moment, but he had to find strength from somewhere. The people in his remaining company had trusted him with their lives. Somehow, he needed to put aside his own fierce grief and lead them.

It was Maddie, the deep lines around her mouth showing her exhaustion. But there was something more. A sadness written in her eyes. For one moment, terror and pain seized him.

"Abigail is resting," she said quietly. "She was awake for a few moments earlier."

The horrible fear that had grabbed him by the throat receded, but his heart didn't heed. It still pounded in his chest like the hooves of a horde of buffalo.

"You should go to her."

He was already shaking his head before she finished the statement. He couldn't bear it.

Maddie's expression darkened. "Mrs. Miller passed away a few minutes ago." Alex, Paul and little Jenny had lost their father only yesterday. Now their mother was gone, too.

Hollis strained his ears and thought he could hear children crying over the quiet sounds of a camp just waking up.

"I'll make arrangements for her burial," he said.

Maddie nodded, eyes downcast. A tear slipped down her cheek and she quickly raised one hand to brush it away. He took a longer look at her. She was pale, but he didn't think she'd been affected by the illness.

Her hands trembled. More tears threatened and she blinked rapidly, her lips pinching. "I'm not usually such a watering pot."

He put a hand on her shoulder.

When she inhaled, he felt the slenderness of her shoulder. "I was hoping the wagons—Owen's part of the company would have made the fort last night," she admitted. Her eyes didn't quite meet his.

He felt the hit of hearing his former friend's name. He'd been watching for the other wagons too. Today marked the sixth day since they'd parted ways. Even if Owen and the others had stayed to rest and heal, they should've arrived yesterday. Shouldn't they?

"You need the doc?" he asked.

Her lips formed a stubborn line. "No."

But she still seemed so fragile.

"When was the last time you slept?" he asked.

She started to open her mouth and then pressed her

lips together, shaking her head. She wouldn't say? Or she didn't know?

Worry tangled his gut in knots. Maddie might not have a medical degree, but she had been caring for patients since the beginning of the journey. The company would be lost without her compassionate nursing.

"Go and lie down. I won't hear you argue," he said when she opened her mouth to protest. "You sleep for a few hours. If I see you out of your tent, I'll set a watch on you."

Another tear slipped free, and she gave in reluctantly. He watched her cross the expanse of grass and then slip inside her tent.

Only after the canvas flap closed did he run a hand down his face. What now?

Sixteen lost.

And it was his fault.

He stole another look at the fort as a dry wind fluttered against his face. There had to be soldiers inside who could help them. Even if the fort doctor had no medicine for their illness, having men to help provide food and tote water, feed his company, help care for the ill... it might've made all the difference.

A shrill whistle caught his attention, pulled it toward the east. Galloping hoofbeats soon followed.

Two riders on horseback.

Hollis recognized Leo's horse and his heart went into his throat. He crossed through camp, aware of the couple of men who followed him out from between the circle of wagons.

It wasn't Leo on that horse.

It was Alice. And... Robert Braddock?

They were riding in a straight line toward the fort, but when he hailed them with both arms waving, they changed direction slightly.

Alice reined in as she neared him and was off the horse before the animal had stopped. She threw herself into Hollis's arms. Shocked, he hugged her for a second before she pushed back.

Braddock remained on his horse. He was hatless and hunched in the saddle as if he were seasick. He was as pale as Maddie had just been, but his nose and the bridge of his cheeks were pink from the sun.

"Please tell me you've a doctor from the fort and everyone is recovered." Alice gestured to the circled wagons wearing an expression of hope. One that Hollis hated to destroy.

Sixteen lost.

He shook his head and her expression darkened.

"Your company isn't faring well?" he asked.

He saw the worry in her expression, felt the concern that Braddock seemed to echo from horseback.

"We need help."

He wanted to ask her how it was that she could ask for help when her stubborn half-brother could not.

"Owen and Leo might've been hit the hardest of all," she said, "but every member of my family is ill and—" She cut herself off, shaking her head.

Despair swamped him. He had to clear his throat to get the words out. "The garrison refused to help. Too afraid of getting infected."

Alice's gaze cut to the fort, determination in the set of her jaw. "I don't care. I'll go in there and *make* them help us."

She might be slight of stature, but in that moment, she seemed fierce as a warrior.

"They won't let you in," Hollis said. Determination wasn't a match for firepower, and those soldiers had plenty of it.

"I don't care," she repeated. This time, Hollis caught the glint of tears in her eyes before she blinked them away. She went back to her horse and boosted herself into the saddle.

"They'll send you away," Hollis said to Braddock. Maybe the man would see reason.

Although he had never seen the two interact in camp. There was some tension there in the way Alice carefully avoided Braddock's eyes, the too-long glance at her from the city-slicker. Why were they working together now?

"I'm going where she goes," Braddock said.

And then they were gone. Hollis watched them ride away, out of sight before they reached the buildings of the fort.

It was useless. If Hollis thought he'd get any compassion from the commander, he'd have approached again and again.

Aimlessly, he wandered through the quiet camp. Many travelers still slept. A few made breakfast. Some mothers checked on their children. He stopped outside the wagon where Abigail had been put. He strained his ears but couldn't hear her breathing. Only the solid beating of his own heart in his ears.

If anything, he felt more lost than he had when Dinah had passed. How could that be? He'd loved Dinah with all of his heart.

He wasn't the same man any longer. That much was

certain. He'd grown up. Lost some of the naivety of a man in his younger years. But not all of it. Wasn't there some part of him that had believed he could have Abigail in his life and not lose her?

He should check on her. Cool her head and neck with damp cloths.

But he couldn't bear seeing her fade away, especially knowing that this was his fault.

It couldn't have been that long that he stood there, staring into nothing, questioning everything. Surely not longer than a half an hour. But when he blinked, there were Alice and Braddock riding back on their horses.

And behind them, a line of soldiers from the fort.

He froze until Alice drew up yards away. "We're going back to the company," she said, a fierce victory in her expression. But Braddock looked shifty, somehow.

"All of you?"

She shook her head. "Some of the men will stay and help here."

Relief flooded him. "Thank you."

"Come back with us," she said. "My brothers should never have split the company. Come back and help, and set them straight."

He heard a rustling from the wagon behind him. Was Abigail rolling over? Making herself more comfortable?

"Owen needs you," Alice urged.

"I'll go," he decided. It was better than staying here, losing Abigail little by little.

"I'm going with you." Abigail, shaky but upright, peeking out from the wagon's canvas covering. Her eyes were on Alice. It was Alice who she spoke to, not Hollis.

"I can ride."

Sixteen

"SIT up and I'll remake that pallet for you." Hollis squatted next to Owen who reclined on a pallet in the open air, not far from the campfire the Mason family had shared for the past days.

Owen sent him a look that might've quelled another person, but Hollis remained where he was and waited Owen out.

Owen hadn't spoken one word to Hollis since he and Alice and Braddock and the soldiers had ridden into the camp. Hollis glanced several yards away, to where Abigail's head and shoulders were visible above a blanket strung between two wagons. She was helping a tired and weak Rachel take a bath.

Abigail hadn't spoken to Hollis since their arrival either.

Possibly because he'd been avoiding her at every turn. It was easy. There was much work to be done, and even with the soldiers' help, the work never ceased. Finally, after another couple of days, the tide was turning.

Many pioneers were recovering. Like Abigail, who'd been very ill for twenty-four hours and then recovered quickly. With the improvements, spirits had grown more positive.

Hollis had been adamant that she not overdo it. Including sending someone to insist she go to bed last night. He'd been pleased and relieved when he'd walked past their makeshift camp, and seen her asleep in her bedroll.

He didn't know why God had granted him a reprieve, why God had allowed her to live. But Hollis intended to keep his distance. The farther he stayed from Abigail, the safer she'd be.

Tired of waiting for the stubborn Owen to move, Hollis nudged his arm.

Owen grunted, then reluctantly rolled off of the pallet and onto his knees. He weaved a bit, even though he wasn't standing. Probably lightheaded, though he'd hate to admit to such weakness to Hollis.

Whatever patching up Alice had hoped for hadn't happened. At least not between Hollis and Owen.

Fine. Neither of them had to like this. Just endure it.

Hollis pulled away the old bedding and quickly spread a new quilt. Owen must've been watching from the corner of his eye, because he laid back down as soon as Hollis finished. He must've twisted wrong, because he pushed a hand into his stomach, grimacing.

Still tender. But at least he'd held down some of a mash Alice had made this morning. His fever was lower. At least that's what the doc said.

The baby cried from where she'd been laid in a long wooden crate padded with a quilt. Owen looked like he was going to push up off his pallet, no matter if he felt like death, to get to her.

Hollis clamped his shoulder. "Stay there. I'll bring her to you."

Something twisted up inside him when he cradled the bit of baby in his hands. What might it have been like if his child had lived...?

He didn't have time to dwell on it, not when the three steps to Owen had been crossed and he was handing her over.

As soon as the baby was nuzzled against Owen's shoulder, her little body relaxed and she made a soft sound. Owen patted her shoulder.

Hollis had to look away. He picked up the bowl of broth one of the soldiers had given him. Sat it beside Owen on the pallet.

"Eat." If Owen wanted to speak to him in grunts, Hollis could do that too.

Owen ignored the bowl.

Hollis felt his temper spark, but tamped it down.

"Eat," he ordered. "You need your strength back."

Owen shook his head.

"You're a stubborn man," Hollis muttered, picking up the old bedding. It needed a good wash. Or maybe to be burned.

"I'm not the stubborn one," Owen growled suddenly. "You're the one who can't accept help. No matter how well intentioned."

Hollis shook his head. That wasn't true.

But apparently now that Owen had spoken, the dam was broken. He wasn't finished. "You push everyone away. Leo. Me. August."

Hollis turned his face from Owen's intent scrutiny.

And found himself watching Abigail.

He could only see one of her ears, her upper cheek, her eye, the top of her head, her hair pulled back into a bun. But she was smiling.

He didn't have to see her entire face to know it.

At the sight of her joy, the small sign that she was all right, a minute amount of tension bled from him. She wasn't entirely recovered, but she wasn't on her deathbed.

"You especially push Abigail away," Owen muttered.

Hollis's body jerked. He sent a scathing look at his former captain. "That's none of your business."

"Of course it isn't."

Now Owen lifted the bowl to his lips and took a long slurp. His eyes never left Hollis's.

Emotion rose in Hollis's throat, strong and hot and choking. He wanted to punch the other man. He was spoiling for a fight. But the frustration and grief and anger had no real target—not when Owen was so sick he could barely get up.

At that moment, Alice walked past the wagon, heading for Abigail and the hidden Rachel with her arms full of fabric. She raised her brows. Hollis didn't know if the look was meant for him or her brother.

If only he could walk away, but Owen was watching him with narrowed eyes. Expecting that he'd do just that.

"I'm cursed," he said, voice low so as not to carry to the women. "Are you happy to know it?"

Saying the words aloud made him feel sick.

Owen shook his head in confusion. "What?"

"It's why I lost my wife and child. Why I lost my

cousin. I know it." Hollis tapped his chest with his fist. "Here. I don't know why, but I'm cursed."

Owen looked skeptical. "God doesn't curse his children."

"He made an exception for me."

Some emotion moved across Owen's expression. "Show me a Bible verse that says God curses his children," he demanded softly.

Hollis shrugged, shook his head.

"God sent his Son to earth for the business of breaking chains," Owen said softly.

Abigail's lilting laugh traveled to his ear on the breeze, and he couldn't help glancing her way. The blanket had shifted so that he had a full view of her face. A drip of soap suds was sliding down her cheeks.

Breaking chains.

A beat of hope slammed into his chest with the strength of his heartbeat.

But, "How do you explain my wife?"

Losing Dinah had meant Hollis lost a part of himself, too.

"I can't explain it." If Owen had ignored him or made fun, it would have been easy for Hollis to walk away. As it was, his feet felt rooted to the ground by Owen's serious expression. "Just like I can't explain why Rachel's husband died. Bad things happen. But I know there's a God up there who loves you. He sent his Son to earth to save your eternal soul."

Hollis's ma had taught him that from the time he could talk. Read him the Bible and sang songs he'd never been able to forget.

"God's got a plan for you," Owen said.

Could it be true?

Hollis couldn't understand how losing Dinah was part of that plan. But maybe he didn't have to understand. Maybe he just had to accept it.

Abigail disappeared from sight as the breathless hope grabbed Hollis by the throat.

Had God put Abigail in his life so that Hollis might have a second chance at happiness?

Hollis turned his gaze on Owen, who looked peaked and a little chagrined.

"I was wrong to leave," Hollis said. "I should've listened." He cleared his throat when the words didn't want to come. "I value your friendship, your advice."

"I was wrong, too," Owen admitted. "I'm grateful you came back. And brought help."

Hollis shook his head. "Alice is the one who brought reinforcements."

"How'd she convince them to come?"

Hollis shook his head. "I don't know. The commander wouldn't give me a lick of help. But she and Braddock disappeared into the fort, and when they rode back out, they had soldiers with them." Braddock had been riding beside one of the more senior soldiers. Hollis had a suspicion, but no proof, that there'd been bribery involved.

Owen frowned. But his expression lightened when Rachel appeared from behind the blanket, freshly bathed, her hair wet down her back. Hollis thought, not for the first time, that his friend was a lovesick fool over Rachel.

And he'd be the same for Abigail.

Abigail had turned away, slowly lugging the washtub, Alice supporting the weight on its other side. He'd hurt Abigail with his callous words, by pushing her away.

Was it too late to mend things?

* * *

Distant thunder rumbled. Abigail opened her eyes to the fire crackling with warmth that felt stifling in the dry morning air. This morning seemed the hottest so far, summer nearly upon them. She'd dreamed—

For a moment, she closed her eyes, sinking back into the dream where Hollis had curved his body behind hers, his arm heavy and secure around her waist, his solid presence filling her with warmth and care.

She opened her eyes again, throwing back the blanket.

It didn't matter how real the dream had felt. It was only her imagination.

Hollis hadn't spoken to her once since she'd woken from the fever. She'd caught a long look from him last night, but he'd been busy with some of the men when she'd fallen into her bedroll in exhaustion.

He probably hadn't slept.

Another ripple of thunder. She squinted against the rising sun. The sky was clear—

No.

Stretching her neck had revealed a line of dark clouds building on the far southern horizon. They seemed so far off. A warm wind blew strands of her hair into her face. It'd been so dry and dusty. Just imagining the cool air that hit right before a rain, the drops of moisture that might hit her face...

Or would it be another flash flood like the one she and Hollis had endured together?

She couldn't bear to dwell on thoughts of those days. She stood. Best to ready herself for today's work.

The sticky heat made it uncomfortable to cook over the fire, but she persisted in making biscuits, wiping sweat with her wrist. Felicity appeared in the quiet campsite on the leading edge of the circle.

"Hollis and Owen have agreed that we'll strike out after the funeral."

Felicity had regained some of her color, but she was winded and tired from carrying the two pails of water she'd brought with her. "Hollis rode off with Owen and August a bit ago."

The funeral.

Abigail wasn't sure she could stomach attending the funeral. The grave had been large. They'd lost a dozen pioneers. None had been safe. Not men, women, or children. Young or old. And thinking about standing at that graveside reminded her too pointedly of standing beside her mother's grave.

No doubt it would be expected for the wagonmaster's wife to offer comfort to those who'd lost loved ones. But she had none to give. She felt empty, scraped raw.

"What's the matter?" Felicity was closer than Abigail had realized, offering the dipper from the pail.

Abigail took it, parched but not yet finished with the biscuits and the fire. "Nothing." She lifted the dipper to her lips, wishing she could hide from Felicity's scrutiny.

"You came to help us when you'd barely recovered, but this seems more than exhaustion."

Abigail turned her face away as she handed the dipper back to her friend. This morning it seemed too difficult to find a tune to hum, to find a smile for her friend. "I'm fine."

But Felicity didn't relent. "You don't seem yourself. A newlywed is supposed to be—"

"I'm fine," Abigail snapped. Instantly, she regretted taking that tone with her friend.

"Abigail—"

She whirled at Felicity's hesitant word. "I'm not a newlywed," she blurted. "It isn't a real marriage between Hollis and me."

She'd thought saying the words would be a relief, but she felt only guilt at the shocked confusion on her friend's face. And sadness that it was true.

Felicity shook her head, her brows coming together. "I see the way he looks at you."

She couldn't know how harsh a blow her words were. *I have nothing to give you.*

"And the way you watch him," Felicity went on.

"Hollis married me to keep the peace in camp. To save my reputation. It isn't real. The farce will be over the moment we reach Oregon."

Felicity watched her face too closely. Abigail was afraid of what her friend saw there. And then the stubborn twist of Felicity's lips. "You love him," she stated clearly.

Despair flowed over Abigail as another roll of thunder boomed in the distance. "I wish I didn't."

The words hung there between the two of them, both true and awful.

"He's lost so much," Abigail whispered. "He won't open his heart again. I tried—"

She couldn't allow the emotion out now. Not when folks were already gathering for the funeral. When she was needed to help pack up and move out.

Hurt dawned in Felicity's expression. "Why didn't you tell me?"

Abigail swallowed hard. "I should've. Just... everything hurt. And I've tried so hard to smile through it. To keep working, keep my chin up."

She was startled by the sudden tears that slipped free. "I'm so tired," she admitted. "Tired of being frightened of the future and what it holds. I've been holding on so tightly since Mam passed, years ago. But out here, there's no safety to be found."

Compassion lit Felicity's eyes. "There are no promises in life," she said. "Except the ones given by our Father in Heaven."

Abigail shook her head. Where had God been when Mam had grown sick and died? When Joseph had left? When Mr. Smith had tried to steal her future when he'd stolen her money?

Abigail had been left alone. Left to her own devices to find a new way through.

When she said as much, Felicity's expression showed pity.

Felicity couldn't understand.

"Everything in my future changed," Abigail said. "God took Mam, took Joseph."

Felicity clasped her hand. "Maybe He was giving you a new future."

The words dropped into Abigail's mind like a stone in a smooth pool. Causing ripples all the way down.

Was Felicity right?

Abigail had been desperate and penniless when she'd arrived in Independence. She hadn't known what her future would hold. But Joseph had already provided. Hollis had taken her on, accepted her into the company.

Hollis, who didn't want her.

She swiped at new tears with her apron. Her emotions felt at war.

God *had* provided for her, kept her these many years.

But she'd wanted a future with Hollis.

"Hollis doesn't want me for a wife." Admitting it made more tears flow.

Felicity had tears in her eyes, too. Her lips pressed together before she spoke. "God has a plan for him, too. Maybe you are meant to be the healing he needs."

These wise words from Felicity settled deep inside Abigail's heart. Hollis was burning up from the inside out. Lost to his grief. Could Felicity be right that Abigail was meant to bring him healing? How?

Abigail had gone into this marriage intent on helping him. Her motives had gotten muddled as her feelings for the enigmatic man had deepened.

Loving someone meant wanting the best for them, didn't it? Hollis had suffered—and deserved every good thing he could have.

Could she give selflessly, knowing her heart would be broken at the end of this journey?

Seventeen

LIGHTNING FLASHED, a bright strike flaring through the building clouds in the south.

The storm was heading this way. Hot wind gusted into Hollis's face, offering no relief. He felt a stirring of unease, as if they might face a flash flood like before, but he reminded himself the company was on a plain, not down by the riverbed where there might be flooding.

From up ahead, August motioned to his right from the back of his horse. Hollis leaned down to see the crushed grass that might mean a horse had passed this way.

It might've also meant a deer. Or buffalo. Or wandering cow.

August had felt well enough to go scouting this morning but had returned to camp quickly, asking Hollis and Owen to accompany him.

Now August reined in, Hollis and Owen just behind him. The two men had resolved their differences and it felt good for Hollis to be able to trust his captain again, even if his other personal concerns remained unresolved.

What had August found? The remains of a campfire—abandoned quickly.

"Up on the bluff," August pointed to the embankment a half-dozen yards above.

The three of them tromped up the incline to the small plateau that created an overlook.

August went on, "There's a place where it looks like he laid on his stomach and watched our camp."

Owen sent a concerned glanced to Hollis. "You were right about someone following us. He's been careful to cover his tracks—until now."

"If he's after the ruby, why didn't he come into camp while everyone was sick?" August wondered aloud.

"He's cautious," Hollis mused. "Maybe he was biding his time. Left when the soldiers rode in."

Owen wore a look tinged with appreciation. "I guess that's another reason to thank you for coming back."

Hollis paced away, scuffing his boot through the grass, looking for any clue the man might've left behind.

"Maybe we can convince Collin to just give it to him," August said to Owen, their voices carrying to Hollis as he moved all the way to the edge of the bluff.

There was a clear view into camp from here. Would be more detailed if the man following them had a pair of field glasses. If he'd spent days camped here, watching, he'd have had time to note all the watches, see the family relationships, know everything about them.

"How would that work?" Owen asked skeptically. "Besides, it's Stella and the girls you'd have to convince."

The jewel didn't belong to the Fairfax women, but it'd ended up in their possession. Hollis would be happy to be rid of it. He didn't need anyone chasing them for the piece of stone stolen from a wealthy Eastern family.

Lightning struck again, lighting up the entire sky, even the side the clouds hadn't covered. It jagged straight to the ground, followed by a boom of thunder so loud it seemed to shake the ground beneath them.

One of the horses whinnied.

Hollis had to blink against the haze of light that wanted to remain in his eyes. "We'd better get back. We'll want to wait out the storm before we travel, especially if it floods—"

He cut himself off, his eyes on the horizon.

Owen had been saying something to August, but now moved to stand at Hollis's side.

"You smell that?"

The wind seemed to carry a tinge of smoke.

Hollis's heart began to pound. An orange glow lit the horizon, spreading fast.

Heading their way.

"Wildfire," August breathed.

The three men didn't look at each other before they were scrambling down the incline and running for their horses, the animals prancing nervously. The stillness, the heavy air, wind blowing right in their direction. The smell of smoke had already intensified.

Several birds flew overhead, startling Hollis's horse as he stepped one foot into the stirrup. He clung to the saddle horn as the animal sidestepped, finally settling into the seat.

"Can we get into the river?" Owen shouted as they took off for camp.

"It's too dangerous. If it floods, the wagons could be swept away." The river was deep and curved near this section. But the danger of being on the plain was even more terrible. All it would take was one spark tumbling on the wind to catch a canvas on fire.

They couldn't outrun it. The wagons, the cattle, the people—the fire was too fast. Already he felt choked by the smoke.

Were they doomed to lose everything? Had he put Abigail and the rest of the company in danger, risked her life all over again?

He let the still small voice inside him confront the swirling fears.

God wasn't against him. He had his captains at his side. And Hollis was going to fight.

What could stop fire? Water. Dirt to smother it. Lack of fuel.

"We need to start a fire burning in a line toward the north," he shouted to Owen and August. "A break wide enough the wildfire can't jump it."

He detailed his plan in their last paces to reach the wagons. As they neared, all three men dismounted at a run.

Owen shouted for Leo as he ran off in one direction. August went the opposite way, gathering help. Fearful faces immediately confronted Hollis when he strode into the circle of wagons.

"The men are needed on the north side of camp," he ordered. "Every man, as long as you're strong enough to walk. Light a torch. Now!"

Thankfully, no one questioned him. They exuded only a determination to survive and faith in Hollis, who'd come back to help when the sickness had overtaken them.

He only hoped he deserved it.

He let his gaze roam the women around camp, those who'd gathered close.

There. Abigail watched with terrified eyes from near August's wagon.

"Find as many buckets, barrels, and pails as you can. Any of you who can walk or run, come and fill them at the river."

Fear pushed the travelers into motion, pails clanking.

He joined Abigail. "Are you all right?" he asked urgently.

Surprise lit her expression, quickly banked. "Yes."

She couldn't hide the shock when he took the washtub from her hands. "Grab those," he nodded to the two pails in the back of the wagon.

Then he grabbed out two of the quilts that were within arms' reach. "Take blankets," he shouted to the nearest women. "We'll soak them in the water."

He threw the blankets over his shoulder and stuck by Abigail's side as she hurried out of camp and toward the water, two in a steady stream of people attempting to save their lives and possessions.

He glanced over his shoulder and saw the men lighting patches of the ground on fire. The wind was working against them, but the men had formed a line and fought with shovels and blankets to keep the fire to the north of their camp.

The break fire licked up the dry grasses, moving more slowly toward the oncoming blaze.

When he went over the lip of the riverbank, he could no longer see them.

Abigail slipped as she scrambled down the bank, landing hard on her backside. He dropped the washtub to grasp her elbow and help her stand. Their gazes caught for a prolonged moment. And then they were off again, running across the muddy bank to the water.

Hollis didn't care that his boots and pant legs got soaked as he filled the washtub as full as he could and still carry it. He pushed both quilts under the water and then slung them around his neck, water streaming down his body. The river was rising, beginning to churn and froth.

Abigail was still weak from the sickness. She struggled with her pails. "Go on," she told him.

He shook his head. "I won't leave you."

For a fractured second, he thought she understood that he meant the words for more than just this moment.

When she'd regained her footing and began to tote the full pails toward the bank and up the incline, he followed her closely with the washtub in his arms.

She broke down coughing halfway to the circled wagon, the acrid smoke burning every breath now. He couldn't let down his tub, but he angled his body so that he blocked what he could of the wind.

Urgency fueled him, but he waited until she looked up at him, tears streaming from her eyes. Moisture flowed down his own face, too, as his eyes burned.

He gave directions and each woman relayed them down the line, around the circle. Women scrabbled to take down the canvases from their wagons, to flatten the tents to the ground. Thank God so many had begun to pack up, ready to move out.

The cattle bawled, several cowboys working to keep them in a bunch, keep them from bolting away.

He grabbed his handkerchief from his pocket and

doused it in the tub, then presented it to Abigail. "Tie it over your nose and mouth."

Her hands were trembling too much to complete the task, and he moved closer. She didn't protest when he gently took the fabric from her fingers and tipped her head back to tie it behind.

Awareness slipped over him amidst the chaos in camp. This was the closest they'd been since the kiss he hadn't taken. "I wish I'd kissed you before," he said.

He saw the flash of surprise, but the moment was wrong. He tied on a bandana of his own before directing her to move in front of the wagon.

"Can you help me put the quilts over the wagon?" he asked, the words muffled through his face covering. He threw the sopping wet quilt over the supplies in the bed of the wagon. She was shaking and dropped the corner of the quilt when he flipped his side up.

He wished he could stop and just hold her. They'd run out of time soon enough. In this moment, he had to keep going. But he found a song inside him and let loose with a cracking voice.

"Deep river, my home is over Jordan..."

She froze, staring at him, but then gripped the edge of the quilt and helped him cover the inside of the wagon. Within a few moments, her faltering voice joined his song, just like he'd heard his mother sing it.

"Lord, I want to cross over into campground..."

A cough broke Abigail's dear voice. Smoke was low and thick, covering everything. He couldn't see the men in front of the wagons anymore.

"It's almost here!" someone cried.

There was a roar in his ears—the roar of the fire.

He curled his arm around Abigail and guided her around the back of the wagon. It would offer them scant protection if the fire crossed the line of burned grass where the men had done their best to form a break.

They huddled there, his arms around her, her face tucked into his chest. He prayed, the words falling from his lips and into her hair as she clung to him.

He didn't know whether his hasty plan was going to work. Maybe he'd doomed them all.

Only God knew.

* * *

Abigail had never known terror like this.

Or the feeling of being held, protected, in stark contrast to everything happening around them.

Something had changed inside her when Hollis began to sing, his voice sure and strong. Hollis couldn't mean it the way it felt for him to hold her like this. To stay by her side when she'd been fearful and clumsy.

Thunder rolled again, louder than the fire roaring close. Heat licked her exposed skin. Choking smoke made every breath burn.

"It worked!" That might've been Owen's shout, but she couldn't be certain. She couldn't even tell its direction from her place tucked in Hollis's embrace.

Slowly, she peeked over Hollis's shoulder. The wildfire had passed by. A huge swath of flames on either side of their caravan, burning the prairie beyond. But not one of their wagons had caught fire.

Cheers rang out from pioneers, interspersed with coughing.

And still Hollis didn't let go of her.

A moment of breathless quiet, then the sky opened up and a deluge of rain descended. Soft, full rain that soaked into the parched ground.

Hollis's arms loosened around her.

Women raced to reattach the canvases to their wagons in hopes of keeping their supplies somewhat dry.

"I should—" She couldn't finish the statement for the coughing fit that took her. She stepped away from him— only to find him stepping closer, offering his hand beneath her elbow to support her.

The rain chased the fire... and then caught it. More smoke furled as the fire was doused inch by inch. More cheers broke out, interspersed with sobs from young children and fits of coughing from everywhere around.

Tears streamed from Abigail's eyes, both from the soot in the air and from relief. She didn't dare look at Hollis, though she was comforted by his closeness.

Her elbow stung where she'd scraped it when she'd fallen near the river. She didn't realize she was holding her other hand to it until Hollis gently tugged her fingers away.

He let go when a man shouted, "Hollis!"

He was needed. He always would be.

But he didn't take the opportunity to run away.

He waved off the man. "I need a minute to tend to my wife."

Tend to my wife.

The words made her belly swoop low, even though she knew he didn't mean them. She tugged the kerchief down from her face, let it lie around her neck. She was already drenched, but the water felt fresh. Cleansing. "I'm all right."

He stood so near there wasn't space to look away from his intense gaze. "I'd like to see for myself."

He tugged her fingers away from her elbow and gently pushed up her sleeve. The soft touch stung.

"You've scraped it," he said. "I'll fetch some ointment."

Someone else called for him. He didn't even look their way.

"It'll keep," she said.

She couldn't understand his tender treatment, not after the way they'd left things. And new tears spilled from her eyes, tracking slowly down her cheeks.

After a breathless moment of hesitation, he gently cupped her cheeks in his hands, wiped her tears away with his thumbs.

"I'm sorry," he said softly. "This hardly seems the time or place to say it, but I can't wait."

He looked so serious, his eyes burning into hers with an intensity she recognized from their time together.

"I'm sorry for many things, but especially for pushing you away all this time. I've been fighting my feelings for you —and," he chuckled wearily, "it hasn't done any good."

A beat of hope stole the air and made her breathe a laugh too.

Hollis continued to hold on to her as people exclaimed joyfully around them.

"Your resourcefulness, your kindness, your optimism, all of it drew me from the very first moment."

Was he really saying this? She'd tried to protect her heart and now it seemed hard to believe.

He wasn't finished. "I felt everything... so deeply." He inhaled, his throat worked.

Rain streamed down, but she couldn't look away from

him. She knew what he'd been through. How much he had lost. How the fragile feelings must've terrified him.

"I'm finished letting fear rule me. If you can find it in your heart to forgive me—"

"Of course I can."

Joy lit his eyes from deep inside. Still, a vulnerability remained.

There were shouts from somewhere outside the little circle of herself and Hollis. She vaguely heard someone else make a shushing noise. Or a shooing noise.

All she could see, all she could hear, was Hollis.

"I want our marriage to be real," he said. "You had the courage to demand of me what I should've given from the beginning." He hesitated. "That is, if I'm not too late."

He seemed genuinely worried that she would reject him. She couldn't bear to leave him in suspense. "You aren't too late."

Everything else seemed to fade away as he pulled her into a proper embrace, as his head dipped and he captured her mouth with his.

His lips were warm and tender, his kiss both familiar and new. His embrace felt like coming home.

His mouth moved from her lips to her jaw, her cheek, then her forehead.

"I've wanted the right to do this," he murmured into her hair, still holding her close. Her arms clung to his sides.

"I love you, Abigail Tremblay," he whispered.

She went completely still.

Had she imagined the words? She'd wanted to hear them so badly...

She needed to see him, to look into his face. When she

pushed against his chest, he loosened his arms so that she could peer up into his eyes.

He looked both frightened and mulish, his chin jutting out as if daring her to contradict him, while his eyes held a vulnerability that echoed inside her.

"I love you, too," she said. "I tried not to. I know you didn't want a second wife, after losing Dinah."

"I did want you for my wife," he admitted. "Only I was afraid of losing you too. When you got sick, I felt so lost— that's how I knew the strength of my feelings."

Rain dripped down his face, but when he wiped one hand over his eyes and cheeks, she guessed that perhaps there were a few tears mingled in.

Love swelled inside her, full to bursting. Her husband had such a tender heart, a strong heart to protect those under his care.

God had given her this man. A new future. It stretched before her, full of endless hope.

Eighteen

ABIGAIL SAT with Ben at a makeshift table in camp outside of the fort. She held Molly, Owen and Rachel's baby, in her arms as the babe slept.

Ben was scowling at the primer on the barrel in front of her as she sounded out, "K-i-t-n. Kitten." Her legs swung like two pendulums above the ground, at different rhythms and speeds.

She turned her scowl on Abigail. "Why do I have to do this?"

"It's good for you." And Felicity and August, who had adopted the little girl weeks ago, had asked for Abigail's help finding something to distract Ben. Ever since the wild-fire, she'd been jumpy and close to tears.

Abigail understood. It'd been two days since the near-disaster. The wagon train had been reunited late this morning and would pull out this afternoon—all as one, together.

Spirits were high. But every time Abigail turned her head just right, she got a whiff of smoke that still clung to parts of the canvas or wood and a frisson of fear spiked through her. She whispered a prayer and let a moment of reflection clear it.

Molly had no such worries. The baby was deeply asleep, content as Abigail held her on her shoulder.

Abigail patted the baby's back, the warm bundle in her arms igniting hopes and long-buried dreams.

"M-i-t-n, mitten," Ben blurted, focus back on the primer.

Abigail caught sight of Alice hauling an armful of quilts between two wagons. The young man who'd ridden with her to the fort—Robert?—approached from the direction of that structure.

When he called out to Alice, she started. When he offered her something—Abigail couldn't make out the bundle in his hands—Alice shook her head. And then Alice made a sharp motion with one hand before clutching the quilts again. Abigail couldn't hear what she said, but she didn't look happy. She climbed into a wagon and Robert was left standing there, alone.

He waited for a long moment, then dropped his head and turned to leave.

"What's this word?" Ben's question interrupted Abigail's focus on the strange drama in front of her. She leaned over Ben's shoulder and helped her sound out the word "mother."

Ben peered up at Abigail. "When're you and Hollis goin' to have a baby? Then you'll be a mother."

At that moment, Hollis passed between two wagons and into her line of sight. Abigail found that her gaze went to him naturally, aware of him even across the camp.

His eyes came up, locking with hers as a smile curled his lips.

You'll be a mother.

Ben's innocent words sent faint heat into her cheeks.

Since the fire, Hollis had been completely different with her. Gone were the walls he'd kept in place, the tight control meant to protect himself—and keep her safe, too.

Last night, he'd needed to meet with some of the captains until late, but he'd taken the time to come to her at the campfire after supper and say goodnight. He'd taken great pleasure in wrapping one strong arm around her waist and kissing her until she'd been breathless and clinging to him.

She'd been asleep when he'd come to his bedroll well after dark, but she'd drowsily felt his tender touch as he adjusted the blanket on her shoulder.

This morning, she'd woken to find herself tucked into the shelter of his embrace. His arm around her middle, her head pillowed on his shoulder.

He'd been awake, the sun already peeking over the horizon, but he'd stayed to hold her. He hadn't run off like before.

She couldn't wait to reach Oregon and have time that was theirs alone. Sleepy mornings sitting across the kitchen table. For now, she'd be content with smiles from across camp, dinners together, and stolen moments.

"Mrs. Abigail, when?" Ben prompted.

The moment of connection with Hollis broken, Abigail turned her attention back to the girl.

"It will happen in God's timing," she said. She felt secure in the knowledge that Hollis loved her, that they were going to have a future together. Even though she wasn't sure if he'd want to keep traversing the trail or find a place in Oregon to live.

Felicity bustled into camp, looking much brighter than she had a few days ago. "Are you bothering Abigail?" she asked of Ben.

"Naw." Ben clapped the covers of the book together. "Can I be finished?"

Felicity and Abigail exchanged a look. "When you reach the end of this section," Felicity said.

Ben hung her head. She sent a sly look at her adopted mother. "Didja know Abigail and Hollis 're gonna have a baby?"

Abigail grimaced as Felicity's brows rose and she turned inquisitive eyes on her friend. "Is that so?" she murmured.

Abigail tucked her cheek against Molly's downy head. "In time."

Felicity's eyes narrowed. "Hmm."

Abigail couldn't meet her friend's probing gaze. Everything with Hollis was so new. She hadn't known how to broach the subject with her friend, though Felicity had no doubt seen the change in Hollis herself.

"So it wasn't a farce?" Felicity asked as she passed by with folded laundry from her basket.

"You were right," Abigail admitted. And couldn't help smiling when Felicity expressed her joy with a little squeal.

"About what?" Hollis's voice gave Abigail a start and she straightened as he joined them, coming to stand behind Ben, close to Abigail's side.

"Just women things," Felicity said breezily. Abigail caught the pointed gaze that meant they would talk later.

"Read with me, Hollis?" Ben begged.

"For a minute," he agreed.

Ben sounded out several words, bright and excited under Hollis's attention.

Hollis let his hand clasp Abigail's, his skin warm and rough against hers. She leaned her shoulder into his side.

This moment was everything she could have dreamed of. Her husband by her side, strong and loving.

He corrected one of Ben's pronunciations and she gusted out a heavy sigh.

"Come and get a snack," Felicity suggested from her nearby wagon.

Ben was all too happy to abandon the primer and scampered off.

"There's coffee in the pot," Abigail said to her husband.

"Thanks." Hollis moved to the still warm coals of the fire, lifted the pot, and poured a cup. When he returned to her, he offered her the cup.

She took a grateful sip and handed it back to him. When he drank from the same place her lips had touched, his eyes met hers above the rim. There was an intimacy to the action, something she'd never shared before.

"I've got to go into the fort. Anything you need? I can probably procure some fabric for a new dress." He'd mentioned yesterday that the dress that had gone into the river with her and spent those difficult days in the wild might need to be replaced.

"Won't it be expensive?" she asked. Everything at the forts seemed priced very dear.

"I've lived years of scrimping and saving—and no one to buy for," he said quietly, his gaze never leaving hers. "It'd bring me joy to provide for you."

How could she say no to that? She let the love rising in her chest show in her face. He came near and brushed a kiss on her forehead, leaving the coffee cup where she could reach it.

"Maddie wants to go into the fort," she told him.

His expression darkened with concern, but he nodded. "I'll find her."

There was only one place to look. With the Miller children. The young nurse had been despondent when the children had lost both mother and father to the typhoid. As the pioneers had needed less care, Maddie had been consumed with caring for the children's needs.

"What will happen to the children?" she asked Hollis now.

"I don't know yet."

She felt the weight of the responsibility on his shoulders. Saw the way he swept his hat off his head and ran his hand through his hair. "Maybe there'll be a family at the fort that can take them in."

Abigail remembered Maddie holding the youngest child, still a toddler, wrapped in a blanket this morning near a campfire. How would Maddie feel if the children were left with a family here?

"I don't know your favorite kind of candy," he muttered as he mashed his hat back on his head.

Her brows quirked. "You don't need to spend any money on candy, sir."

His eyes narrowed slightly. "It seems like the kind of information a husband should know about his wife."

Wife. The word spoken in a teasing growl settled in her heart.

She stood and brushed off her dress, reached up and planted one more kiss on his cheek. "If you must know, lemon candy always makes me smile."

He cupped her cheek for a moment and then let her go. "I'll be back soon."

"I'll be waiting. Husband."

She watched him cross camp. Beyond their safe circle of wagons, the prairie stretched as far as she could see. Enormous. And wild.

There's a rugged beauty to it, Hollis had said so many days ago, when they'd been alone and lost. She knew that in a few weeks, they'd discover tall mountains waiting for them, a breathless beauty she couldn't yet imagine. What would the future hold? She couldn't know, but with Hollis at her side, she would face it with courage.

* * *

Hollis and a handful of other travelers were approaching the fort on foot when he noticed another group of wagons sending up a plume of dust. They weren't moving very fast, and he watched for a moment as they began to circle up.

It was a smaller group, and from what he could see, the oxen looked exhausted, dragging. Was the wagonmaster pushing too hard?

"More travelers?" Maddie asked from where she walked a couple of yards away.

"Seems so."

Maddie's eyes skittered over the other wagons and Hollis's mind drifted to Abigail. Where it seemed to want to go every waking second, whether he had business to attend to or not.

Husband. She'd been teasing, but there was a seriousness to the way she'd used the word as a claim.

She was his wife. He was her husband.

Forever.

Everything with her seemed so natural that it felt ridiculous that he'd fought against being with her for so long.

Being with her was easy. It was good. Frighteningly so.

He'd woken this morning from a nightmare where she'd been ripped away from him in the wildfire. It'd taken several minutes for a clear head to prevail, for him to remember the promises that Owen had helped him come to terms with. Remember the goodness of God, who'd brought them together.

It was getting easier to believe in the future he so dearly wanted.

Business complete inside the fort, he joined his fellow travelers at the store, which was crowded and loud.

"Are you the wagonmaster?" A man approached, his hand extended for a handshake. "I'm Will Thatcher. My wagon's been here for ten days for an axle repair. The company my family was traveling with left us behind and we're looking to join up."

For the first time, Hollis noticed a little girl clinging to the man's leg.

Thatcher caught Hollis's curious glance and put his hand on the girls' head. "We lost her mother." he cleared his throat. "Three weeks ago."

"I'm sorry to hear that. We're pulling out in two hours," Hollis said. "One of my captains can meet with you to go over the company rules."

The man nodded with a grateful look, though his smile didn't meet his eyes. Compassion stirred. What a terrible thing to go through.

Hollis found the bolts of fabric and Maddie fingering a

calico. She glanced up, then past Hollis. He looked over his shoulder and caught sight of Braddock, who was speaking to a uniformed soldier. As Hollis watched, Braddock slipped several dollar bills into the man's hand.

"Wonder if he mentioned his bribery to Alice," Maddie muttered.

Hollis raised his brows at her.

"He couldn't have convinced the soldiers to come and help us any other way," she said matter-of-factly. "Probably kept it a secret. I myself think it was sharp and efficient. Got us the help we needed."

But Alice wouldn't. Alice was known for her upright morals. Maddie was probably right. Braddock had been tight-lipped about how he'd convinced soldiers to help. Alice didn't seem to know.

Hollis chose a sprigged gingham and had several yards cut for Abigail, imagining the gentle joy on her face when she saw what he'd chosen. He was browsing the glass jars filled with candy when a voice from the past spoke somewhere in the near vicinity.

"—flour so expensive in all my life."

He turned on his heel, his breath caught in his chest.

Peter.

He hadn't seen his brother, two years younger, for several years. The brown skin, so close in color to Hollis's own, and dark mop of close-cropped hair beneath his hat were unmistakable.

"Peter?" His voice was rough when the name passed his lips.

His brother jerked, his head coming up. Looking at him was like looking in a mirror, the image slightly distorted.

"You're all grown up," Hollis fought against the hot ball of emotion that lodged in his chest.

"Hollis? Is it really you?" His brother looked as if he'd seen a ghost, but he stepped closer, only barely glancing at the store proprietor who'd been speaking to him.

Hollis couldn't hold back. He embraced his brother. The hold was too short. He stepped back, looking his brother up and down. Peter appeared worn, tired lines bracketing his mouth.

"Are you traveling with the group that just arrived?"

Peter nodded. He watched Hollis with brows drawn, emotion gathering in his expression as if he'd only just realized that his brother was standing before him in the flesh. "I thought to see you in Independence. I wrote."

The hot ball of emotion lodged itself firmly in Hollis's chest cavity.

"I couldn't," Hollis admitted, eyes down. "I'd left behind everything in my life that had been touched by Dinah's presence—"

"Including your family." There was a touch of anger in Peter's voice.

"I was wrong to do it." Hollis could see now how deeply he must've hurt his family. "I just... couldn't." He shook his head. Realized they were surrounded by curious patrons, shopping and meddling and listening.

"I'm sorry," he said. "I've missed you." Love for his brother washed over him. Another piece of his life that he'd walled away.

Peter seemed to soften. "The journey has been more difficult than I anticipated. On Phoebe and the children, too."

Children. Peter was married, and had children.

"Can I meet them?" Hollis asked. "I'll bring my wife."

A short time later, he approached the new ring of wagons with Abigail at his side.

Nerves had tied his stomach in a knot, and he couldn't seem to unhinge his jaw or relax it. Or let go of Abigail's hand where he clung to it.

She knew. She jostled their linked hands back and forth. "Everything is going to be fine."

He found her words more reassuring than her telling him not to be nervous. His brother had seemed more amicable toward him by the time Hollis had left him in the store, but he couldn't predict what Peter might say when they came face to face again. Maybe having more time to consider what he'd felt seeing Hollis, Peter might've found his anger again.

Firelight flickered between wagons as Hollis and Abigail approached.

"Uncle Hollis!"

"Unca!"

Two young voices cried out. A boy of about four darted between the conveyances toward them. A second boy, who couldn't have been older than three, toddled behind him.

The boy threw himself forward, forcing Hollis to let go of Abigail and catch the boy in a half-hug, half-hold.

A woman's laughter rang out, and his sister-in-law was silhouetted in the firelight.

"Phoebe," his voice caught again. She'd been five years younger the last time he'd seen her, fresh-faced and so in love with his brother.

Now she looked happy but weary. And she was pregnant with another child.

"Introduce me to your wife, brother." That was the bossy young woman he remembered.

He and Abigail were dragged to the family campfire, where introductions were made all around. Abigail took it all in stride, laughing and smiling with the children, a little shy when introduced to his brother.

Hollis found himself sitting on a crate, with little Elijah on his knee, while Milton regaled Abigail with tales of a weird animal he'd encountered in the woods.

"It sounds terrifying," Abigail said, wide-eyed.

"Tewwifyin'," Elijah echoed.

"Will you settle in Willamette Valley?" Peter asked.

Hollis glanced at Abigail, who was focused on the children but had turned her face slightly to indicate she'd heard the question as well.

They hadn't spoken of the future, not beyond the commitment to honor their marriage vows. "Abigail's brother is waiting for her in Oregon," he said. "We'll want to spend some time with him before we make any definite plans. Abigail has her heart set on starting a bakery."

Phoebe seemed impressed at that idea. Abigail sent him a quick beaming smile before Milton grabbed her hand and stole her attention again.

"It would be lovely to end up as neighbors," Phoebe said.

Hollis looked at his brother, who nodded. "It's been too long since you've been a part of the family."

"Agreed," Hollis said quietly. "If you've a mind to come alongside, there's room for you in our company."

"Not that you'll see Hollis," Abigail teased. "He's busy morning to night charging his captains with the safety of our travelers and seeing to the needs of everyone."

The clear pride in her voice echoed in Peter's expression. His heart was full, watching his wife interact with his nephews. Finding his way back to his family.

God had given him this gift of restoration. Of a new future, one that Hollis never would have chosen but now didn't see how he could live without.

DOC HAD WAITED until Hollis was nearly ready to pull out before he visited the fort's store. He didn't favor crowded spaces, but there was nothing for it now. He needed more medicines to refill his store, badly depleted after the epidemic.

And as he glanced at the shelf of tonics and tinctures on the wall behind the counter, he found himself sorely disappointed. He wouldn't find what he needed here.

His throat soured. Without access to the right medicines, he would be limited in ways to help the pioneers in Hollis's wagon train.

"And this, please." The familiar feminine voice came from his left side, farther down the shop's counter.

Maddie.

She hadn't seen him yet. From where he stood, a pile of items on the counter partially blocked his view, but there was no mistaking the fiery head of hair.

It took a moment, but he realized that the haphazard pile of children's shoes, fabric, pots, and foodstuffs belonged to her. That she meant to purchase it. What was she doing?

The shopkeeper bustled out from behind the counter and into the store proper as she waited. A couple of men in soldier's uniforms entered and began to browse.

He should leave. Doc doubted the shopkeeper had any other store of medicines. But he couldn't make himself go without asking, and the man was tied up with Maddie.

Her gaze idly skimmed her purchases—and then bypassed them and landed on Doc.

He saw the flash of recognition. And the immediate turn of her head in the opposite direction.

She doesn't know what she's doing. She'll put the travelers in your company in more danger.

He'd said the words to Owen, not knowing she was near enough to hear. It was only after he'd seen her stricken expression that he realized his voice had carried.

Now he needed to do the right thing. His feet carried him to stand next to her pile of things on the counter. "I'd like to apologize."

Before the wagon train had split, he'd worked in close quarters with her. *I'm sorry*, he'd heard a man groan when Maddie cleaned away his shirt covered with vomit. A woman had sobbed the words when Maddie, with an arm around her, guided her into the woods to urgently relieve herself.

In both instances, Maddie had been compassionate and kind, her patient bedside manner and smile unwavering. He understood why the travelers in Hollis's company respected and leaned on her so much.

But at his own apology, he did not receive one of her

smiles. She kept her face averted completely. "That isn't necessary," she mumbled.

"Yes, it is. I'm sorry for what I said." He caught sight of her reflection in the wavy mirror behind the counter.

Her lips pinched with displeasure. "You may be sorry for saying the words aloud, but we both know that you meant them."

Her cool tone covered a show of temper. He was certain of it. He'd heard the same in Marie's voice on the rare occasions they'd quarreled.

But she was right, though not for the reasons she probably thought.

She was a fine nurse, just not a doctor with a doctor's knowledge.

She was also a distraction that he desperately didn't need.

He was opening his mouth to speak when she turned the full force of her hazel eyes on him. "The prairie is a big place. There's plenty of room in Hollis's company for both of us. I see no reason why we need to speak again."

He should be grateful for the words and their implications. She'd stay away from him if he stayed away from her. But her dismissive manner—and perhaps the idea of never speaking to her again—sparked his own temper.

The proprietor approached her from this side of the counter, catching Maddie's attention. "Is there anyone who can help me cart these purchases to my wagon?" Her warm smile was engaging.

"I'd be happy to, miss." The young soldier doffed his hat with an eager smile and an attentive manner.

"Is all this for your family, then?" the soldier asked.

"Yes." Maddie had turned her warm smile on him and

Doc saw how the young man's shoulders straightened. The twinkle that lit in his eye.

"Your husband didn't come along to help you?"

"I don't have a husband," Maddie said sweetly.

She hadn't looked at Doc once since she'd spoken to the soldier.

The young man's face brightened.

Something ugly twisted low inside Doc's belly.

"I'll need just a moment to complete my purchase," she said.

But the proprietor had been distracted by a more mature soldier, pulled to the other side of the room where they spoke in low voices.

"I don't believe those shoes will fit your sister," Doc said. Maddie had two adult sisters and those were obviously a pair of children's shoes.

"Who is all of this really for?" he pushed when she ignored him.

"My children," she said coolly. "I've taken charge of Alex, Paul, and Jenny."

Surely she couldn't mean she was taking them on permanently. *My children*, she'd said.

"You can't." He regretted the hastily spoken words when her eyes flashed at him.

"They've no one else." She ground out the words.

He stood for a moment as the thought of young, unmarried Maddie taking on responsibility for three young children settled.

It wasn't right. Surely there was a family among Hollis's company that would take them.

Doc was aware of the handsome soldier hovering nearby, listening to their conversation.

He couldn't seem to look away from Maddie, just like he couldn't seem to stop himself from arguing with her. "You can't mean—"

"I assure you, I do." She turned her face to him, finally, her chin set in a stubborn way he'd come to recognize.

"It's foolhardy."

That was definitely a spark of temper in her eyes. "It's none of your business."

Of course it wasn't. But she was going to ruin her life in this foolish endeavor. "You cannot possibly handle three young children. How will you feed them?"

At that, a flash of uncertainty passed through her expression, quickly masked. "We'll make do."

"What about when you reach Oregon? How will you provide a shelter over their heads?" he pushed.

"We'll make do," she said stubbornly. "I love them."

As if that simple fact meant anything in such a cruel world. She was naive and misguided.

She put him out of sorts.

"You are the most infuriating person I have ever met." The words escaped before he'd thought them through.

She stared at him through narrowed eyes—he hadn't realized they now stood almost nose to nose. Surely he hadn't been the one to lean in.

A string of tension tightened between them. For a breathless moment it all seemed to hover in the air. The inappropriate attraction he couldn't seem to drown, her naivety, the hopeful spirit that life hadn't sucked away. So why did part of him want to take her in his arms and protect her from all of it?

A throat clearing broke the antagonizing moment

frozen between them. The proprietor moved behind the counter. "Can I help you, sir?" he asked Doc.

Who'd turned toward him instinctively, shaken by the fractured moment of closeness.

It took a prolonged minute to steady his voice. "Do you have any other medicines?" he gestured to the shelf behind the man, who shook his head.

Fine.

What a worthless endeavor. Just like attempting to convince a stubborn young woman not to ruin her life.

As he turned away, Maddie stared straight ahead. But he still heard her murmured words. "Perhaps it is too much to hope that I never see you again."

Doc strode through the store and out into the evening air. Her parting sentiment hit him like a blow.

What had he done? He'd meant to make a simple apology, but somehow she'd tied him up in knots and he—he hadn't meant to devolve into that argument.

She was right. What business of his was it if she ruined her life by taking charge of those children?

Being around her wasn't healthy for him. His racing heart and the anger still coursing through his veins was enough evidence of that.

He'd abide by her wish. He'd stay as far away from her as possible.

* * *

Thank you for reading A RUGGED BEAUTY. I hope you loved Hollis and Abigail's romance. You'll see them again in LOVE'S HEALING PATH...

Maddie Fairfax may be young, but on this Oregon-bound wagon train, the pioneers welcome help from the self-trained nurse. Until Dr. Jason Goodwin joins up with their company. The doctor portrays a frosty exterior, but Maddie may be the only one who sees the profound loneliness that haunts him.

After losing his wife and children in a terrible accident, Jason has vowed not to open his heart again. But when Maddie takes on the care of three young orphans, Jason finds himself entangled in the lives of the makeshift family. And as their journey west continues, Maddie's radiant compassion begins to light up the darkest corners of his heart.

Until the unthinkable happens. Will Jason's guarded heart and Maddie's untamed spirit pull them apart?

ONE CLICK LOVE'S HEALING PATH NOW >

For my Family.

A note from the author

A mutual friend introduced to my (now) dear friend Benita at a church event. This mutual friend knew I was an author and knew Benita loves to read. And I mean, LOVES to read. It didn't take long for Benita to ask me, "have you ever written about an African American character?" I had to admit that I hadn't—and that conversation stuck with me for a long time. I didn't have a good reason why I'd never written an African American hero or heroine.

That conversation several years ago sparked the idea for this book. I did quite a bit of research—and I'm certain I didn't do these characters justice, even though I did my best. This book did pass through a sensitivity reader. If mistakes remain, they are entirely mine.

Benita, I want to thank you for challenging me to be more inclusive in my writing. Everything I've learned while writing this book will go with me into future books.

Acknowledgments

Benita, I love your questions when you read early drafts of my books. Your insights make each book better, and I so appreciate your keen mind!

As always, I'm grateful to my proofreaders Lillian, MaryEllen, Benecia, and Shelley for helping me clean up all the little errors (there were many!)—and do my early/advanced readers who caught even more that snuck through. A million thanks!

A special thank you for my readers

With special thank to my readers. You inspire me, you challenge me, your emails and reviews make me smile. This book is for you.

Thank you for picking up not just this book, but the ones that came before it. Whether you've been with me from the start or just joined, your support is truly appreciated.

I hope you can escape into these books, find love, recognize parts of yourself in the courage and tenaciousness of my characters.

With sincere thanks to (listed in alphabetical order by first name:

Abby Johnson, Agnes P, Alesha Diane Oliver Lane, Alicia Bunting, Alissa Burns, Amber Kraker, Amy Kathleen Shippy, Andi P, Angela Eugenia Yotter Vogelman in memory of, Angela Sunaga, Angeline Farrow-Douglas, Anita Leonore Homberger Schaer, Anita Say Holquist, Ann Badder, Ann Stromsness, Anna A, Anna Krug, Annette, April Adams, Araceli Martinez, Araina, Ashley Lankford, Autumn McClain, Ava, Barb Blauvelt, Barb DeNamur, Barb Motz, Barbara Raymond, Barbara Van Norman, Barbara Weintz, Becky Boyce, Becky Cole, Benita J. Jackson, Beth Lewis, Bethany Mabin, Betty Larson, Bettye Short,

BeverlyAnn, Blanchediane, Bobbie Sue Brown, Bonny D. Rambarran, Brenda K Coulter, Brenda v green, Brenda Witt, Bridgette K. Shippy, Bronwyn, Brooke Elizabeth, Carla Illikainen, Carmen Jacob, Carol KOBEL, Carolyn Bryant, Carolyn Mary, Cassandra Garcia, Cate VanNostrand, Catherine, Cathy Whittington, CC O, Celia Miller, Charlene Hammonds, Charmaine Tan, Cheree Lynn, Chris Meiser, Christa Richmond Gruener, Christine M.Knapp, Christine Wikoff, Cindy Fetner, Cindy Rosinski, Cindy Van Hoose, Cricket the cat, Crystal Bufford, Crystal Stewart, Cynthia Keene, Daisy, Dale McCorvey, Darla J Stapleton, Darrell Grimley, Dawn M. Medlock, Dawne Itnyre, Deanna W, Debbie, Debbie Gallagher, Debbie Hammer, Debbie J Roberts, Debbie L, Debbie Meers, Debi Rylander, Deborah Blocher, Deborah Brandel Mansfield, Deborah Gould, Deborah L Crawshaw, Debra Fiest, Debra Rylander, Debra S, Debra Shelton, Dee Olson, Dellas Anderton, Denise Colby, Denise Marx, Diane, Diane T Moore, Donna Duke, Donnalyn Flory, Eddy Cash-Dudley, EJ Derenzy, Elaine Kiefer, Ellen Siler, Emily Catherine, Erin, Esther Searcy, F.Diane Davis, Faith Fryman, Fran Scruggs, Frances Hampton, Frances Scruggs, Gail Estes Hollingsworth, Gaynl Smith, Genevieve Greever, Georgine, Ginger Cilny, Ginny Butterfield, Grace Katherine Peterson, Grace Louise Newton, Heather Schnackenberg, Heidi Hamstra, HeidiLorin Callies, Irina A, JackieT, Jacquie A, Jamie Wagnor, Janet La Grasta, Janet Orta, Janet Ruth Balcomb, Janice Agnew, Janice J Grogan, Janice Montoya, Jasmine M., Jean, Jean Weiser, Jeanne Wright, Jeminka <3, Jenn C., Jennifer Fuller, Jennifer R Woody, Jessica Letourneau, Jessie L Bell, Jim Schroeder, Jo ☺, Jo Ellen McDonald, Jo O'Brien, Joanna Barker, Joanna Westbrook,

Jodi Shadden, Joelle Cutino, John K., Joyce M, Juanita Garcia, Judi Calvert, Judith, Judith DeBoer, Judy Sexton, Judy Snyder-Howe, Judy Voight-Wong, Julie Bell Wadsworth, Julie Standifer, June L. Nelson, Karen Zimmerman, Kathy Adamski, Kathy Cook, Kathy McCauley, Kathy Schlagel, Kay R, Kelly Jo Yaksich, Kim Barrett, Kim Wells, Kimberley Buck, Koni Kodes, Krishnee, Kristen Faro, Kunita R. Gear, Lana Hicks Burton, Laura Delgado, Laurianne Hyder Murphy, Laurie j Thames, Leona, Linda, Linda Helen, Linda K. Duncan, Linda L., Linda Oliphant, Linda Wilber, Lisa A. Lagnese, LK Layne, Lora Musikantow, Lori Smanski, Lorraine Austin, Lucila, Lucy M Chappell, Lynne, Mandy Bentley, Margaret Fraleigh, Margaret Mitchell, Maria Blodgett, MariaElena, Marian O., Marian Owens, Marina Leonard, Marion, Marlene Moore, Martha J. Malone, Mary Ann Speel, Mary Bridgland Jones, Mary K. Thayer, Mattie Miller, Maureen V., Melba Jean Worley, Melody, Melody Rekow, MeMe Debra P, Michelle Epps, Michelle Rhoden, Michelle Spann, Miranda Grattan, MjHagler, Monique Cocanougher, Nancy L Hall, Natalie N. Jacobs, Natasha P., Nelene Segale, Nina Banks, NonnaD, Norma Burks, OliveL, Pam Belcher, Pam I Am, Pamela C. Overton, Pamela Chandler, Pat Strack, Patricia Bennett Barber, Patricia Martinez, Patti Johnson, Patti Paulhamus, Paula Louise Smith, Paula Thaxton, Peggy Legg, Peggy Mangum, Pete Johanson, Phyllis Willett, Rebecca L. LeDoux, Rebel Lee, Reese West, Renée Jackson, Rhonda, Rhonda Moore, Richard D Kawamoto, Rick Carpenter, Rosa I Colon, Ruthe Threet, Sally Childs, Samantha Day, Sandi Kay, Sandra Phillips, Sandra Thompson, Sandy G, Sandy glunz, Sara White, Sarah DeLong, September Whitmire, Sharon G.

Carbone, Sharon Lee, Sharon Meier, Sharon S., Sharon W. Steward, Shelley Crews, Sherry Felkel, Sherry Kaufmann, Sherry Troutman, Shirley, Shirley Hackman, Shirley J. Minnie, Shirley Lawrence, Sondra Weaver, Staci Gomes, Sue R, Sue Roskos, Sue White, surelygoodness, Susan Ellingwood, Susan Evelyn, Susan Nikolaus, Susan Nuss, Susie Brownback, Suzette M Davis, Suzy Yates, Sylvia Pollet, Tabitha L, Terrie Harwood, Terry McGaha, Theresa Stanton, Tina Rice, Tina Shannon, Tracie Smith, Tricia Lee, Trinity Womack, Trixi Oberembt, Valri Western, Vernona Hale, Vicki Meredith, Vida V Arrington, Viola FrereMartin, Virginia Campbell, VIVIAN PEARSON, Vona Ogren, VONDA R. EGGLESTON, Wanda L Schwoerer, Wendy Valle, Wilma Smith

Want to connect online? Here's where you can find me:

GET NEW RELEASE ALERTS

Follow me on Amazon
Follow me on Bookbub
Follow me on Goodreads

CONNECT ON THE WEB

www.lacywilliams.net
lacy@lacywilliams.net

SOCIAL MEDIA

Her Convenient Cowboy

Her Cowboy Deputy

Catching the Cowgirl

The Cowboy's Honor

Winning the Schoolmarm

The Wrangler's Ready-Made Family

Christmas Homecoming

Heart of Gold

SUTTER'S HOLLOW SERIES (CONTEMPORARY ROMANCE)

His Small-Town Girl

Secondhand Cowboy

The Cowgirl Next Door

COWBOY FAIRYTALES SERIES (CONTEMPORARY FAIRYTALE ROMANCE)

Once Upon a Cowboy

Cowboy Charming

The Toad Prince

The Beastly Princess

The Lost Princess

Kissing Kelsey

Courting Carrie

Stealing Sarah

Keeping Kayla

Melting Megan

The Other Princess

The Prince's Matchmaker

HOMETOWN SWEETHEARTS SERIES (CONTEMPORARY ROMANCE)

Kissed by a Cowboy

Love Letters from Cowboy

Mistletoe Cowboy

The Bull Rider

The Brother

The Prodigal

Cowgirl for Keeps

Jingle Bell Cowgirl

Heart of a Cowgirl

3 Days with a Cowboy

Prodigal Cowgirl

Soldier Under the Mistletoe

The Nanny's Christmas Wish

The Rancher's Unexpected Gift

Someone Old

Someone New

Someone Borrowed

Someone Blue (newsletter subscribers only)

Ten Dates

Next Door Santa

Always a Bridesmaid

Love Lessons

NOT IN A SERIES

Wagon Train Sweetheart (historical romance)